*"I can jus_____
are scrolli_____, he
said, a definite edge to his voice.*

She smiled, unable to resist taunting him. "I doubt that you can."

"Why don't you give me a chance to tell my side of the story?"

"Because I'm not interested in anything you have to say." She started to move past him, but he caught her arm.

The jolt of heat that shot through her veins in response to the contact was as unwelcome as it was unexpected. She had to wonder what it said about *her* that the briefest touch could send her pulse racing. It was as if she were hard-wired to respond to this man as she'd never responded to anyone else before or since their long-ago affair.

His fingers uncurled. His hand dropped away. "Of course not," he said sardonically. "It's just about selling papers, right?"

"That's my job," she reminded him.

Dear Reader,

Gabriella Vasquez and her "Dear Gabby" column were originally created to introduce the Reigning Men series on eHarlequin. She was only supposed to be a promotional tool, not a heroine. I certainly had no intention of giving her a story of her own.

But as Gabby wrote her columns, there was a common thread in her responses to readers—an animosity towards the prince regent's cousin, Cameron Leandres. And who could blame her? In the original series, he tried to usurp the throne from Prince Rowan and he put the moves on Prince Marcus's girlfriend—and almost every other female in sight.

Still, Gabriella's aversion to the prince seemed deeply personal, and I began to wonder: What could have happened to make her dislike him so much? And I began to worry: Could I make this prince into a hero?

Because obviously there was some kind of history between these two characters...and it was a story I needed to tell. *The Prince's Second Chance* is that story—I hope you enjoy it!

Best,

Brenda Harlen

THE PRINCE'S
SECOND CHANCE

BRENDA HARLEN

SPECIAL EDITION®

Published by Silhouette Books

America's Publisher of Contemporary Romance

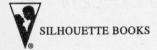 SILHOUETTE BOOKS

ISBN-13: 978-0-373-65582-3

Recycling programs
for this product may
not exist in your area.

THE PRINCE'S SECOND CHANCE

Copyright © 2011 by Brenda Harlen

Visit Silhouette Books at www.eHarlequin.com

Printed in U.S.A.

Books by Brenda Harlen

Silhouette Special Edition

Once and Again #1714
*Her Best-Kept Secret #1756
The Marriage Solution #1811
†One Man's Family #1827
The New Girl in Town #1859
**The Prince's Royal Dilemma #1898
**The Prince's Cowgirl Bride #1920
††Family in Progress #1928
**The Prince's Holiday Baby #1942
*‡The Texas Tycoon's
  Christmas Baby* #2016
‡‡The Engagement Project #2021
‡‡The Pregnancy Plan #2038
‡‡The Baby Surprise #2056
§Thunder Canyon Homecoming #2079
**The Prince's Second Chance #2100

Silhouette Romantic Suspense

McIver's Mission #1224
Some Kind of Hero #1246
Extreme Measures #1282
Bulletproof Hearts #1313
Dangerous Passions #1394

*Family Business
†Logan's Legacy Revisited
**Reigning Men
††Back in Business
‡The Foleys and the McCords
‡‡Brides & Babies
§Montana Mavericks:
  Thunder Canyon Cowboys

BRENDA HARLEN

grew up in a small town surrounded by books and imaginary friends. Although she always dreamed of being a writer, she chose to follow a more traditional career path first. After two years of practicing as an attorney (including an appearance in front of the Supreme Court of Canada), she gave up her "real" job to be a mom and to try her hand at writing books. Three years, five manuscripts and another baby later, she sold her first book—an RWA Golden Heart winner—to Silhouette Books.

Brenda lives in southern Ontario with her real-life husband/hero, two heroes-in-training and two neurotic dogs. She is still surrounded by books (too many books, according to her children) and imaginary friends, but she also enjoys communicating with "real" people. Readers can contact Brenda by email at brendaharlen@yahoo.com or by snail mail c/o Silhouette Books, 233 Broadway, Suite 1001, New York, NY 10279.

In memory of Catherine Elizabeth Witmer
~writer, reader, reviewer & friend~

Chapter One

"Do you have a minute?"

It wasn't every day that Cameron Leandres looked up from his desk to find Rowan Santiago, his cousin and the prince regent of Tesoro del Mar, standing in the doorway of his office.

"Of course," Cameron said, because he couldn't imagine responding in any other way to the ruler of the country. "But not much more than that—I'm meeting with the Ardenan Trade Minister at nine-thirty."

"Actually, that meeting has been…postponed," Rowan told him.

Cameron frowned. "No one told me."

"I just got off the phone with Benedicto Romero."

He immediately recognized the name of Ardena's king and waited silently, apprehensively, for his cousin to continue.

"He's furious about this morning's paper and threatening not to renew our trade agreement."

"I skimmed the front section," Cameron said. "I didn't see anything that would impact our negotiations."

"Did you check the society pages?" The prince regent tossed the paper onto his desk.

The photo and the headline battled for his attention, but it was the bold words that won out: *Prince Cameron Adds New Notch to His Bedpost?*

It was a mockery of the headline that had run on the front page only a few days earlier, *Prince Cameron Adds New Title to His Portfolio*, announcing that he'd been named the country's new Minister of Trade. He didn't want to know what *this* article claimed, but his eyes automatically began to skim the brief paragraph.

Apparently his new responsibilities on the political scene haven't curbed the prince's extracurricular activities. In fact, just last night the prince was spotted at Club Sapphire making some serious moves on the dance floor—and on the King of Ardena's youngest daughter.

Cameron clenched his jaw, holding back the vehement curse that instinctively sprang to his lips. He glanced at the photo again, recognizing the woman who had plastered herself against him on the dance floor.

"I didn't know that she was the king's daughter," he said, ruefully acknowledging that truth wasn't much of a defense.

"The king's seventeen-year-old daughter."

Cameron dropped his head into his hands, and this time he didn't manage to hold back the curse.

"Did you sleep with her?" Rowan asked bluntly.

"No!" Maybe he shouldn't have been shocked by the question, but he was. And while he might have told anyone else that it wasn't their business, he couldn't say that to the prince regent. They both knew his actions reflected on his office.

He was relieved to be able to assert his innocence in this situation, because even if he hadn't guessed that the woman in the photo was underage, he had known that she was far too young for even a serious flirtation. While he hadn't always been discriminating in his choice of female companions, he was thirty-six years old now and long past the age where he was easily seduced by a warm body and willing smile.

"I was there with Allegra de Havilland," he explained, naming his frequent if not exclusive companion of the past six months, "and this girl—she only said her name was Leticia— came up to me on the dance floor while my date was in the ladies' room. We didn't even dance for two minutes. When Allegra came back, she and I left."

His cousin nodded. "Then there's no reason to believe that this can't be salvaged."

Cameron didn't know how to respond. His cousin had taken a chance on him six years earlier when he'd first appointed him to his cabinet, after Cameron had done everything in his power to undermine Rowan's position. At the time, he'd suspected that Rowan was subscribing to the old adage "keep your friends close and your enemies closer" and he couldn't blame him for that. But over time, as they'd worked together on various projects, they'd developed a mutual respect for one another. And Cameron would forever be grateful to his cousin for giving him the chance to be something more than a worthless title in the history books.

When he finally spoke, it was only to say, "I regret that this has caused a problem with the king."

Rowan nodded. "You need to be extra cautious and remember that, as a royal and a member of public office, everything you say and do is subject to media scrutiny."

"Do you want my resignation?" He held his breath, waiting for his cousin's response.

"No, I don't want your resignation. You've been an asset to this administration."

Cameron exhaled. "Do you want me to talk to the king?"

"No," Rowan said again. "I've invited him to join me for lunch. Hopefully I can smooth things over with him then."

Cameron refused to consider what the repercussions might be if his cousin failed. Rowan hadn't been born for the position he was in, but he'd stepped in without missing a beat when Julian and Catherine, his brother and sister-in-law, were killed in a fluke explosion on their yacht.

Maybe Cameron had resented Rowan's appointment back then, because he'd felt that he was just as qualified and capable of doing the prince regent's job. But over the past half-dozen years, he'd realized that he didn't want those duties and responsibilities, even on an interim basis. And he regretted that his own actions—however inadvertent—were making his cousin's job more difficult.

"I also contacted *La Noticia,*" Rowan continued. "Because I was annoyed that Alex would run such a headline without at least giving us a heads-up."

Alex Girard was the society columnist for the local paper whose fair and objective reporting had earned him several invitations to the palace and the opportunity to write exclusive stories about the royal family. Now that Cameron thought about it, it wasn't only out-of-character for the reporter to launch an attack on a member of the prince regent's cabinet but potentially detrimental to his own career.

"As it turns out, Alex didn't have anything to do with the story. He's out of the country for a couple of weeks so the society pages are being covered by another staff writer— Gabriella Vasquez."

Cameron should have guessed that. Not that she'd always hated him. In fact, there was a time when they'd been extremely close. But that was long before she'd become "Dear Gabby" and started using her column to vilify both his character and his activities. And while her references to him had always been unmistakable, she was usually more subtle in her condemnation. Now she'd apparently taken the gloves off.

And he was prepared to do the same.

* * *

Gabriella wasn't surprised when she received the summons to her editor's office, but she did feel the tiniest twinge of guilt when she saw Allison Jenkins—one of her oldest and dearest friends—rubbing her forehead, as she often did when a major headache was brewing.

"You wanted to see me?" Gabriella said.

The editor looked up. "I'm sure you know why."

"Since there wasn't anything particularly controversial in my 'Dear Gabby' column this week, I'm guessing this is about the 'Around Town' segment."

"Would you also like to take a guess as to how many phone calls I've received this morning? Or how many emails have flooded my inbox?"

Gabriella's own office computer had actually been so over-loaded with incoming messages that it had crashed, but she was unconcerned. Everyone knew that the newspaper business was suffering and anything that increased circulation—as her contribution to the society pages had done exponentially—couldn't be a bad thing.

"So put your big girl panties on and deal with it," Gabriella said. "That's why they pay you the big bucks."

Alli shook her head. "You're not even sorry."

"Why should I be? I didn't write anything that wasn't true."

"You may have created an international scandal," her editor warned.

"*I* wasn't dirty dancing with the King of Ardena's underage daughter," she pointed out.

"They were dancing," Alli repeated. "There is absolutely no evidence of anything more than that."

"I never said that there was."

"No," her boss agreed. "But your text implies that the prince is a seducer of virgins."

Gabriella knew that he was, but she didn't intend to admit

that to her boss. "Royal headlines sell papers," she reminded Allison.

"And we get a lot of inside news because we've worked hard to establish a good relationship with the palace."

"Do you really think anyone at the palace even noticed an article buried in the middle of page twelve?"

"I don't think it, I know it," Alli told her. "Because one of the multitude of phone calls that I received was from Prince Rowan."

Gabriella swallowed. "The prince regent called you?"

"And he wasn't very happy."

"Then I'll apologize for putting you in an awkward position," she said. "But I can't apologize for what I wrote. Prince Cameron uses his title and his charm to lure women into his bed and innocent girls should be forewarned."

"Then take out a public service announcement with your name on it but don't use this newspaper to pursue what is obviously a personal vendetta."

Gabriella felt the sting of that reprimand because she knew there was some truth in her boss's words. When Alex Girard had asked her to cover the celebrity watch while he was on vacation, she'd had mixed feelings about the request. For the better part of sixteen years, she'd been careful to steer clear of anyone connected with the royal family. Of course, that hadn't been too difficult for a commoner who didn't move in the same circles they did.

But this new assignment would require Gabriella to seek them out, to go to the places they were known to frequent, to rub elbows with their friends and acquaintances. Of course, the assignment was broader than the royal family, but everyone knew that the Santiagos and the Leandreses were the real celebrities in Tesoro del Mar.

"For Monday's paper, I wrote about the prince regent's picnic at the beach with his family. Tuesday, I covered Princess Molly's book launch and her reading at the library. Yesterday,

I was out of town interviewing the Hollywood elite who are filming a romantic comedy in San Pedro. In fact, I didn't even want to go to Club Sapphire last night, but I got a tip that 'several people of note' were going to be there, so I went."

"Who else was there?" Alli wanted to know.

"Most of the Hollywood contingent," Gabriella admitted.

"Why didn't you get any pictures of them?"

"Because I already have a ton of photos that were taken during the interview sessions."

Alli dropped her head into her hands. "Are you trying to give me an ulcer?"

"I did my job," Gabriella said.

"Which you could have done just as effectively by concentrating on the visiting actors—what they were wearing, what they were drinking, who was hooked up with whom."

"And ignoring the prince's presence?" Gabriella challenged.

"It would have been enough to reference the fact that Prince Cameron was there," her editor insisted.

"With the king's daughter," Gabriella reminded her.

"I'm going to end up with an ulcer and a pink slip," Alli muttered. "But at least I'll have you to keep me company when I'm unemployed."

"I didn't cross any lines."

"Tell that to the legal department when we get slapped with a libel suit."

"It's not libelous if it's true," Gabriella insisted.

"But the truth is often a matter of opinion, isn't that correct, Ms. Vasquez?"

Gabriella recognized that voice. Even after more than sixteen years, the smooth, sexy tone hadn't faded from her memory, and her breath caught in her throat as she spun around to face the door.

Cameron.

"This day just keeps getting better and better," Alli grumbled, but not so loudly that the prince could hear.

Gabriella didn't see her friend move—she couldn't seem to tear her eyes from the man lounging indolently against the doorjamb—but she heard the chair slide and knew that Alli was rising to her feet in deference to the man at her door. She would probably even curtsy.

Gabriella refused to do the same. She wouldn't bow and scrape to this man. Not now, not ever again.

But she couldn't deny that seeing him made her heart slam against her ribs, and while she was determined to play the scene out coolly and casually, her knees had gone just a little weak.

He hadn't changed much in sixteen years. His hair was still thick and dark and slightly tousled, as if he couldn't be bothered to tame it. His golden-brown eyes were further enhanced by thick, black lashes and bold, arched brows. His perfectly-shaped and seductively-soft lips were now compressed in a firm line, the only outward sign of his displeasure.

He was dressed in a charcoal-colored suit with a snowy white shirt that enhanced his olive skin and a black-and-silver patterned tie. But in his case, it was the man who made the clothes rather than vice versa, and not just because he was a royal but because of the supreme confidence he wore even more comfortably than the designer threads on his back.

On closer inspection, she realized that there were some subtle signs of the passing of time: a few strands of gray near his temples, laugh lines fanning out from his eyes, but certainly nothing that detracted from his overall appearance.

His shoulders seemed just as broad as she remembered; his body appeared as hard and lean. He'd always known who he was, what he wanted, and he'd never let anything—or anyone—stand in his way. He was as outrageously sexy and devilishly handsome as ever, and she'd never stood a chance.

"Do you think we could speak privately in your office?"

Cameron asked her, his tone as casual as his posture—and in complete contradiction to the anger that she saw glinting in the depths of those hazel eyes.

Gabriella lifted her chin. "I don't have an office, I have a cubicle. Not all of us are handed cushy jobs with—"

"You can use mine," Alli interrupted hastily, shooting daggers at Gabriella as she moved past her on the way to the door. "I have to get to a meeting with the marketing director, anyway."

"Thank you," Cameron said, inclining his head toward her.

Gabriella had no intention of thanking her boss. She was feeling anything but grateful at the prospect of being stuck in Allison's tiny little office with a man who had always made her feel overwhelmed in his presence. But she squared her shoulders, reminded herself that she wasn't seventeen years old anymore, and faced him defiantly.

In the more than sixteen years that had passed since he'd dated Gabriella Vasquez, Cameron hadn't forgotten about her, but many of the details had faded from his mind. Facing her now, those details came flooding back, washing over him in a powerful wave that left his head struggling to stay above water.

When they'd first met, her hair was a tumbling mass of curls that fell to the middle of her back. Now, the sexy sun-streaked dark tresses grazed her shoulders and the shorter style drew attention to her face, to the dusky gold skin, cocoa-colored eyes, long, inky lashes, and soft, full lips that promised a taste of heaven.

His gaze drifted lower. From her full, round breasts to a narrow waist and the subtle flare of slim hips and down long, lean legs. His hands ached to trace the familiar contours as they'd done so many years before, and he had to curl his fingers into his palms to resist the urge to reach for her.

But even more than her physical attributes, what had attracted him was that she had spirit and spunk—even when she knew she was outgunned, she didn't surrender. From the first time they met, she'd been a challenge—and an incredible pleasure. He pushed aside the memory, firmly slammed the door on the past.

"Sixteen years is a long time to hold a grudge, wouldn't you agree?" he asked her.

"I would," she said easily. "And while I realize you may find this difficult to believe, the page twelve article wasn't about you."

He snorted, confirming his disbelief.

"The 'Around Town' section of the newspaper covers celebrity sightings and rumors. I saw you at the club with Princess Leticia and it seemed obvious to me that royalty hooking up with royalty would make some pretty good headlines."

"So it was just about selling papers?"

"That's my job," she said pleasantly.

"Why don't I believe you?"

She shrugged. "I've been writing an advice column for *La Noticia* for twelve years—my editor could confirm that fact, but you scared her away."

He felt a smile tug at the corners of his mouth, but refused to give into it. "Maybe because your editor has more sense than you do."

"Maybe," she agreed.

"You don't think I could have you fired?" he challenged softly.

Her eyes flashed, but her tone remained even when she responded. "I'm sure you could, but then I would have to sue for unlawful termination and all the gory details would be revealed, putting far too much importance on one little article."

His gaze narrowed. "That 'one little article' may result in

the King of Ardena walking away from a trade agreement that has been in place for more than fifty years."

"That would be unfortunate," she said, "but hardly my fault."

"You implied that I seduced his daughter."

"Did you?" She held up her hands. "Sorry. Forget I asked. I don't want to know and it's none of my business."

He gritted his teeth, but before he could respond, the ring of a cell phone intruded.

"Excuse me," she said, turning away from him to check the display on the slim instrument he hadn't realized was in her hand. Frowning, she connected the call. "Sierra?"

He couldn't hear what the caller was saying, but judging by the way Gabriella's face paled, the news was not good.

He was more than a little annoyed with her, irritated by her easy dismissal of him, and furious about the headlines she'd manufactured. So why did seeing the obvious distress on her face bother him? Why did he wish she would turn *to* him rather than turn away?

Gabriella's hands were unsteady as she closed the phone. The call had obviously shaken her, but when she turned back to him again, her face was carefully composed.

"As fascinating as this conversation has been," she said lightly, "I have to go."

"We're not done here, Gabriella."

She lifted her chin in a gesture that intrigued him as much as it irked him. "If you have any other concerns about the job I'm doing, take them up with my editor."

He let her brush past him and head out the door, and he tried to ignore the regret that gnawed at his belly.

There was no point in wishing that he'd handled things differently sixteen years earlier, no point in wondering where they might be now if he had. He'd been given more than enough second chances in his life; he couldn't expect another one from Gabriella.

And even if he wasn't still royally ticked about her creative reporting, she'd made it more than clear that she had no interest in him whatsoever. Not that he was entirely sure he believed her claim. Because if she truly didn't have any feelings for him, why did she continue to target him in her column? Why had she written a headline that she had to know would get his attention?

I did my job.

Her words echoed in his mind and he wondered if it really was as simple as that. Maybe he only wanted to believe that she'd never forgotten about him because he'd never forgotten about her.

They'd dated for only a few months, and although he'd dated a lot of other women both before and after his brief affair with Gabriella, no one else had ever lingered in his mind the way she had done.

She'd been both naive and inexperienced—and not at all his type. But there was something about her innocence that tugged at him, something about her purity and sweetness that had thoroughly captivated him.

She hadn't been similarly entranced. While a lot of women had wanted to be with him because he was a prince, Gabriella had seemed more intimidated than impressed by his title— and determined to keep him at a distance. But he'd never been the type to take a detour just because someone had set up a roadblock, and that was an aspect of his personality that hadn't changed in the past sixteen years.

No, Gabriella, he thought as he followed her path out the door. *We're not even close to being done.*

Chapter Two

Gabriella was still shaking as she exited through the automatic doors and stepped into the bright sunshine, but she knew it wasn't Sierra's phone call alone that was responsible for her distress. Learning that a child was in the hospital would be enough to send any parent into a panic, but hearing her daughter's voice had reassured Gabriella somewhat. Of course, she wouldn't be completely reassured until she'd held Sierra in her arms, so she unlocked the door and sank into the driver's seat, anxious to get to the hospital to do just that.

She tried to put Cameron Leandres out of her mind as she drove, but her thoughts were torn between worry for her daughter and worry for herself—and the secret she'd been holding on to for sixteen years.

It was her own fault. She should have realized that there would be repercussions if she continued to taunt him in print. But she'd been so angry with him for so long, and when she'd seen him at the club, up close and personal for the first time in so many years, she'd been overwhelmed by memories and emotions. And then she'd seen him dancing with the young Ardenan princess, and she'd recognized the look on the teenager's face when she'd gazed up at the prince because she'd once looked at him exactly the same way.

And for just a little while, Cameron had looked back at Gabriella as if she was the center of his world, and she'd let herself believe that she could be. She'd deluded herself into trusting that he truly cared about her, that she actually mattered to him. She wasn't the first woman to make that mistake, and she certainly hadn't been the last, though that knowledge didn't lessen her heartache in the slightest.

But that was a long time ago, and she was over him, wholly and completely. And if her heart had done a funny little skip when she'd seen him standing in the doorway of Allison's office, well, that wasn't really surprising. He was still an incredibly attractive man and any woman would have responded the same way. In fact, she'd be willing to bet that even Alli's cynical heart had gone pitter-patter. Not that she was going to question her editor about it. In fact, if she never again heard his name from her friend's lips, it would be too soon.

But just as she pulled into the hospital parking lot, her phone beeped to indicate an incoming text message. She drove into a vacant spot and checked the display.

where r u? r u with the prince? i came back to my office and u both were gone and i picked up some pretty heavy vibes btwn the 2 of u.

So much for thinking she might be able to avoid the topic, but it was easier to lie to her friend when she didn't have to look her in the eye. So she texted back:

I got a call from Sierra. She was in a fender bender with a friend. I'm at the hospital now, will check in with you later.

Then she tucked the phone in her purse, put both Allison Jenkins and Cameron Leandres out of her mind, and went into the hospital.

"Sierra Vasquez?" she said to the nurse behind the desk.

"First room on the right, third curtain on the left."

"Thank you."

She found her daughter exactly where the nurse had indicated. She looked so small and pale on the narrow hospital cot, the fluorescent yellow cast on her arm a bright contrast to the pale green sheets on the bed. Her heels clicked on the tile floor as she crossed the room, and Sierra's eyes flicked open.

"Hi, Mom."

"Hi." She brushed a dark curl off of her daughter's forehead and touched her lips to the pale skin there. "You told me you weren't hurt."

"I'm not," Sierra said. "Not really. And I didn't want you to freak out."

"Do I look like I'm freaking out?"

Sierra's lips tilted up at the corners. "I know when you're freaking out, even when no one else does."

"Well, it's a mother's prerogative to worry about her child." She pulled a chair up beside the bed. "How's Jenna?"

"Not a scratch. Her mom came and got her already. Mrs. Azzaro wanted to wait to see you, but she had a deposition or something that she had to get back to court for."

"I'll call Luisa tonight," Gabriella said, and took Sierra's hand in hers. "So what happened?"

"A cat ran across the road. Jenna swerved to avoid it and ended up hitting a lamppost."

"I didn't even know Jenna had her license," she noted.

"She got it three weeks ago," Sierra admitted.

"And her parents let her drive to school?"

"Probably the first and last time."

"Probably," Gabriella said. "Although I'm sure Don and

Luisa are just as relieved as I am that no one was seriously injured."

"I wish I could say the same about the car."

"Cars can be fixed," Gabriella said.

"Speaking of fixed," Sierra said. "Why are you all fixed up today?"

Gabriella glanced down at her matching skirt and jacket. She'd always told Sierra that one of the greatest advantages of working from home was being able to work in her pj's. Not that she usually did so, but she also didn't dig "the good clothes" out of the back of her closet or torture her feet in three-inch heels except for rare visits to the newspaper offices.

"I had a meeting with my editor this morning."

Her daughter's brows rose.

"Don't ask," Gabriella told her.

"I'm sorry if I dragged you away from something important," Sierra said.

"Nothing is more important than you." She put her arm across her daughter's shoulder, hugged her carefully. "And I don't think I need to point out that this accident wouldn't have happened if you'd been at school, where you were supposed to be."

"I had a free period, Mom."

"During which you're supposed to do your homework or study."

"Jenna wanted to get a new pair of shoes for her date with Kevin tonight and there was a sale..." her explanation trailed off when she caught the look on her mother's face. "Okay, I won't leave school property again without getting your permission first."

"And to make sure you remember that, you're grounded for a week."

"A week?" Sierra squawked indignantly.

"Are you angling for two?" Gabriella asked.

Her daughter sighed. "Okay—a week."

Gabriella stood up again. "Now I'm going to find the doctor to get you out of here, then we'll go rent some movies and spend the night—"

"You're not staying home with me tonight, Mom."

She frowned. "Why not?"

"Because Rafe's flying in for the weekend, and he said he was going to make reservations at L'Atelier." Sierra frowned at her. "You forgot, didn't you?"

"No," she denied, although not very convincingly. But she hadn't forgotten so much as she'd pushed the information to the back of her mind, not nearly as excited about Rafe's plans as her daughter seemed to be.

"This could be the night," Sierra continued, "and I'm not going to be the one to screw things up for you."

She didn't need to when Gabriella was perfectly capable of screwing things up entirely on her own, and probably would. But she wasn't going to think about that now. She wasn't going to worry about what might or might not happen with the American businessman who had started dropping hints about the future he wanted for them together.

"Honey, Rafe and I can have dinner another time. I don't want you to be alone tonight."

"Paolo could come over to watch movies with me."

Gabriella raised her eyebrows. "And I certainly don't want you alone with your boyfriend."

Sierra rolled her eyes. "I didn't expect we would be alone—Grandma will be home, won't she?"

Still, she hesitated.

"I only broke my wrist," Sierra said. "That's no reason for you to break your plans with Rafe."

"Rafe will understand."

Sierra sighed. "Mom, he's going to ask you to marry him tonight."

"He didn't tell you that, did he?"

"No, but I'm not an idiot. An impromptu visit, dinner at L'Atelier, something important to discuss..."

No, her daughter definitely wasn't an idiot. And Gabriella knew she should be pleased that Sierra obviously liked and approved of the man her mother had been dating for the past year and a half. Of course, everyone liked Rafe. He was a wonderful man—handsome and successful and generous and giving, and Gabriella cared for him a great deal. But marriage?

She was almost thirty-four years old and she'd lost her innocence a long time ago, but she was still relatively naive and inexperienced. She'd fallen head over heels in love only once, when she was barely seventeen years old, and her life experiences after that had been very different from most other girls her age. She'd survived first love and first heartbreak, but it had taken her a long time to put the pieces of her shattered heart back together.

While she'd long ago abandoned her girlish dreams of walking down the aisle, she'd believed that her heart was sufficiently mended that she could fall in love again. But as wonderful as Rafe was—and he truly was—something still held her back.

She refused to let herself think about what that something—or who that someone—might be.

Cameron didn't feel like going out. After being ambushed by the underage princess at Club Sapphire the night before, he wanted only to stay home, far away from the prying eyes of the paparazzi.

Maybe he was getting old. Since his thirtieth birthday, more than six years ago, he'd started to think that he wanted more than an endless parade of interchangeable women through his life. Spending time with friends and family members who were happily married had further convinced him that he wanted that same kind of close connection with someone—someday. But it seemed that he could never stay with any one woman long enough to allow that kind of closeness to develop. Or maybe he'd just never met the right woman.

When Michael's daughter was born, Cameron had become even more aware of the emptiness of his own life. The realization that he wanted a family wasn't just unexpected but shocking, considering how screwed up his own family had been.

His father—Gaetan Leandres—had been a farmer by birth and by trade and he'd been content with his lot in life, at least until he'd had the misfortune of falling in love with a princess. They'd married against, and possibly to spite, her father's wishes, and they'd had three children together. Cameron believed that Elena had loved her husband, but when Gaetan had died and left her alone, she'd suddenly resented everything that she'd given up to be with him.

So she'd tried to pass her dreams and ambitions on to her children. Michael, her firstborn, had always known what he wanted and had refused to let her manipulate him. Marissa, her youngest child and only daughter, had mostly escaped Elena's attention by virtue of her gender. So it was almost by default that she'd focused her efforts on her second son.

And Cameron, still looking for his own place and purpose in life, had been much more susceptible to his mother's manipulations. As a result, he'd done some things he wasn't proud of, hurt a lot of people who never should have been hurt, and walked away from the only woman he'd ever loved.

Walked away? His lips twisted wryly. No, what he'd done was push her away—so forcefully and finally that she'd never wanted to look back. And Cameron had never let himself look back, either. He'd never let himself admit that he might have made a mistake, that every woman he'd been with since had been little more than a pale substitute for her.

Until today when, for the first time in more than sixteen years, he'd found himself face-to-face with her again.

Gabriella Vasquez—the only woman who had ever taken hold of his heart.

He closed his eyes, as if that might banish her image from his mind. He didn't want to think of her now, to remember what they'd once shared, to imagine what might have been. There was no point. Gabriella was his past and he had to look to the future.

Not that a status-conscious socialite like Allegra was a woman he could imagine being with for the rest of his life. But hopefully a casual meal with his frequent companion would generate some positive publicity to counteract all the negative headlines of last night's fiasco at Club Sapphire.

And there would be publicity—of that he had no doubt. Gone were the days when he only had to worry about card-carrying members of the media shoving cameras in his face— now they hid in the shadows and used telephoto lenses. And even if no paparazzi were around, there would be someone with a camera in a cell phone eager to snap a shot.

He arrived at Allegra's condo at seven-fifteen, knowing she would keep him waiting at least fifteen minutes. He didn't usually mind, but for some reason, he found the delay to-night more than a little irritating. When Allegra swept into the room, however, he couldn't deny that she was worth the wait.

She was wearing a sheath-style dress of emerald green that molded to her slender frame and enhanced the color of her eyes. Her long, blond hair was styled in a fancy twist that was both sexy and sophisticated. Round emeralds surrounded by diamonds glittered at her ears and a matching pendant dangled between her breasts.

"I'm sorry I kept you waiting," she said.

"You look lovely," he said, his response as automatic as her apology, though probably more sincere.

"Would you like a drink before we go?" she asked, gestur-ing toward the well-stocked bar in the corner.

He shook his head. "We have reservations at L'Atelier and if we don't leave now, we'll be late."

"L'Atelier?" Her eyes lit up and her lips curved as she tucked her hand in his arms. "Aren't you full of surprises tonight?"

When they were seated at one of only a half-dozen tables in the exclusive upper-level dining room, Cameron ordered a bottle of Cristal because he knew it was Allegra's favorite.

During the course of the meal, they sipped the champagne and talked about nothing of importance. When the waiter cleared away his empty plate and the remnants of Allegra's coq au vin—because she never did more than sample her dinner—a flash of color near the doorway caught his eye.

A swirling red dress wrapped around luscious feminine curves. A tumble of dark curls that grazed sexy shoulders. A low, throaty laugh that shot through his blood like an exquisite cognac.

His breath caught; his throat went dry.

No, it couldn't be.

Then she turned, and his heart actually skipped a beat.

It *was* Gabriella.

He didn't recognize the man she was with, but he didn't really take a good look. He couldn't tear his eyes off of the woman who had preoccupied far too many of his thoughts since their encounter earlier that morning—the same woman who had haunted his dreams for far too many years.

She looked absolutely stunning. Sensual. Sexy. Seductive.

The return of the waiter with their dessert dragged his attention back to his own table. He noticed that Allegra was frowning slightly, obviously displeased by the wavering of his attention but reluctant to say anything about it.

He reached across the table for her hand, and she smiled at him. She was always quick to forgive and forget—and willing to disregard troublesome newspaper headlines. It was unfortunate, he thought, that he wasn't even close to falling in love with her.

"Allegra—"

She leaned forward, her eyes bright and filled with anticipation. "Yes?"

He drew in a breath. "I think we should take a break."

She blinked. Once. Twice. "*Excuse* me?"

He couldn't blame her for appearing shell-shocked. He had no idea where those words had come from. And yet, now that he'd spoken them, he felt an immense sense of relief—and more than a little bit of guilt.

"You brought me here tonight...to dump me?"

"No," he said. "I didn't plan— I mean, I'm not dumping you."

Her eyes filled with tears, but she valiantly held them in check. He breathed a silent sigh of relief, grateful that she wasn't the type of woman to make a nasty scene.

"It sure sounds that way to me." Her voice was cool and carefully controlled as she pushed her chair away from the table. Then she picked up her champagne glass and tossed the contents in his face. "You son of a bitch."

So much for thinking she wouldn't cause a scene, Cameron thought, as he wiped up the Cristal with his linen napkin.

Gabriella had escaped to the ladies' room for a moment of quiet to catch her breath and settle her nerves. As she'd readied herself for her date with Rafe, she'd worried about Sierra's prediction. When they'd arrived at the restaurant and been led to the upper level, her apprehension had increased.

She knew there were about half a dozen tables in the exclusive dining room, but the arrangement and décor were such that the diners at each table had the illusion of complete privacy. There were tall columns and lush greenery, soft lights and romantic music, and just walking into the scene had her stomach twisting into knots. Because in that moment, she knew that Sierra was right—Rafe had brought her here tonight because he was going to ask her to marry him, and she didn't know how she would respond to that question.

She considered calling her daughter and begging Sierra to call *her* with some trumped-up emergency that required Gabriella to immediately return home. The only reason she didn't make the call was that she knew she couldn't count on Sierra's complicity. Her daughter clearly thought it was a good idea for Gabriella to marry Rafe and wouldn't understand her hesitation. A hesitation that had led her to hiding out in the ladies' room rather than facing a perfectly wonderful man who wanted to spend his life with her.

As she was reapplying her lip gloss, the door to the ladies' room flew open. When a weeping woman flung herself onto the chaise lounge and buried her face in her hands, Gabriella realized that some people had bigger problems than she did.

She dropped the lip gloss back into her purse and glanced around, but the spacious room was otherwise empty. So she plucked a handful of tissues from the box on the counter and went to the sitting area, lowering herself to the edge of a chair facing the distraught woman.

Wordlessly, she offered the tissues.

The blonde lifted her head, looked at her through beautiful, tear-drenched eyes.

Gabriella barely managed to hold back a shocked gasp.

It had been awkward enough to imagine that she'd been trapped in the washroom with a broken-hearted but anonymous stranger. But she knew who this woman was—she was Allegra de Havilland, Prince Cameron's consort.

As quickly as Gabriella identified the woman, she also recognized that the juiciest headline of her career was in the palm of her hand.

Chapter Three

She immediately pushed the thought aside, ashamed that she would consider—even for a second—capitalizing on someone else's pain for the purpose of advancing her career. It wasn't as if she aspired to take over Alex Girard's "Around Town" column, after all, she was just having some fun with it while her colleague was on vacation. But it would be cruel to exploit Allegra's obvious heartache for a headline. So Gabriella didn't ask what the callous prince had done, she only asked, "Do you want me to call you a cab?"

The gorgeous heiress dabbed carefully at the mascara streaks under her eyes. But instead of answering Gabriella's question, she said, "I thought things were moving along nicely, that we were moving toward being exclusive."

"Men are usually a few steps behind women when it comes to relationships," Gabriella said lightly.

"I could have handled it if he said he needed more time, but he said we should take a break, spend some time apart."

Gabriella winced, understanding how harshly those insensitive words would slice through a heart that was filled with love. On the other hand, they weren't nearly as cold as the words—and the fistful of cash—he'd once thrown at her.

"Everyone warned me that he was a snake," Allegra continued, "but I didn't believe them. I didn't want to believe them, because he was always so considerate and charming."

Calling Cameron Leandres a snake was an insult to snakes, but Gabriella kept that assessment to herself, knowing that it would do nothing to ease Allegra's pain.

"After almost six months, he's suddenly changed his mind about what he wants?" Her eyes filled with tears again. "I want to hate him. There's a part of me that does hate him. But a bigger part really does love him." She dabbed at the streaks of mascara again, then her eyes suddenly went wide. "I'm so sorry—you must have a husband or a boyfriend or someone waiting for you—"

"It's okay," Gabriella assured her. "He won't mind."

"He must be a real prince of a guy," Allegra said softly.

She smiled at the irony. "He really is."

"Then you're a lucky woman."

Gabriella nodded. "So what are your plans for the rest of the night? Are you going back to your date—" she deliberately didn't use Cameron's name or title because she didn't want Allegra to know that she'd guessed his identity "—or do you want the maitre d' to call a cab for you?"

"I can't go back out there. I threw my champagne in his face."

Gabriella nearly choked trying to hold back a laugh. "Then you don't have to," she assured the other woman. "You wait here, and I'll come back to get you when your cab has arrived."

"You're being very kind," Allegra said gratefully.

"I've been where you are," she said, then, taking in the luxurious surroundings, she smiled wryly. "Well, not exactly.

But I've had my heart broken before, so I can relate—at least a little—to what you're feeling right now."

She took a quick detour to where Rafe was seated, to let him know what she was doing before she tracked down the maitre d'. She tried to apologize for the interruption of the romantic evening he'd planned but, Rafe being Rafe, he understood.

After she watched Allegra's cab pull away, she turned—and came face-to-face with Prince Cameron Leandres for the second time that day.

"I can just imagine the headlines that are scrolling through your mind," he said, a definite edge to his voice.

She smiled, unable to resist taunting him. "I doubt that you can."

"Why don't you give me a chance to tell my side of the story?"

"Because I'm not interested in anything you have to say." She started to move past him, but he caught her arm.

The jolt of heat that shot through her veins in response to the contact was as unwelcome as it was unexpected. As low as her opinion was of him, she had to wonder what it said about *her* that the briefest touch could send her pulse racing. Except that her heart had been pounding even before he'd touched her—even before she'd seen him standing there. It was as if she was hardwired to respond to this man as she'd never responded to anyone else before or since their long-ago affair.

But while she couldn't deny her instinctive reaction to him, she had no intention of letting him know the effect he had on her. Instead of yanking her arm from his grasp, as she wanted to do, she simply looked at his hand and lifted her brows, deliberately cool and unaffected.

His fingers uncurled, his hand dropped away. "Of course not," he said sardonically. "It's just about selling papers, right?"

"That's my job," she reminded him, then moved past him to return to her date.

But she was obviously more flustered than she wanted to admit, because as soon as she got back to the table, Rafe was on his feet, his brow furrowed with concern. "Are you okay?"

She forced a smile. "Yeah. It's just been a really long day."

"I ordered pizza," he told her.

She glanced up, startled. "Pizza?"

"From Pinelli's," he explained. "We can pick it up on the way back to your place."

"But—"

He touched a finger to her lips, silencing her protest. "We'll do this again some other time," he promised her.

"I'm sorry."

And she *was* sorry that she'd ruined the mood he'd so carefully set—but she was also relieved that he wouldn't be getting down on one knee tonight.

"Don't be," he said, and brushed his lips against hers.

The gentle kiss was as steady and reliable as the man who kissed her. There was no startling jolt of awareness, no unexpected surge of heat, nothing she couldn't handle. And Gabriella was glad for that. She didn't ever want to feel out of control again.

Rafe tossed more than enough cash on the table to pay for the bottle of champagne they'd barely touched and compensate the waiter for the tip on the hefty dinner tab he was missing out on as a result of their premature exit. Then they picked up two extra-large cheese and pepperoni pizzas on the way home, to share with Sierra and Paolo and Katarina, Gabriella's mother who had canceled her own plans in order to stay home and chaperone the young couple.

In the comfort of her home, surrounded by family, Gabriella found herself relaxing again. And when Rafe said that he was going to call it a night, she exhaled a silent sigh of relief as she walked him to the door. Obviously her suspicions about his intentions tonight had been off-base. As she'd told Allegra, women usually started thinking about commitment before men and Rafe was obviously happy with the status quo.

Or so she thought until he pulled a small, square box out of his jacket pocket.

Her eyes went wide, her breath caught, and she felt a fine sheen of perspiration bead on her brow.

Rafe chuckled, but the sound was strained. "Honestly, Gabriella, I've never known another woman who would blanch at the sight of a jeweler's box."

She swallowed, forced a smile. "I don't like to be predictable."

"No worries there." He flipped open the lid, and her eyes dropped back to the box with the same combination of fascination and trepidation that compelled passersby to gawk at the scene of an accident.

"Wow," she said, and swallowed again.

"I've had this ring for a couple of months now. I brought it with me tonight because I thought—I'd *hoped*—you might finally be ready to wear it." He closed the lid again and pressed the box into her hand. "But I know you're not, so I'm only going to ask you to hold on to it until you are."

She looked up at him, hoping he knew how truly sorry she was that she couldn't take the ring out of the box and put it on her finger. And hoping, just as desperately, that someday she would be ready.

It was with more than a little apprehension that Cameron unfolded his newspaper the next morning. Seeing nothing on the front page that was cause for concern, he turned the page. By the time he got to the "Around Town" section, he was mentally drafting his resignation, certain that nothing he could say or do would save his political career after Gabriella

Vasquez had pried all the intimate details of his latest failed relationship from his obviously unhappy ex-girlfriend. But the headline at the top of the page—*American Actress Storms Off Set*—gave him pause.

Although he didn't usually read the gossip columns, he forced himself to do so now, to ensure that he wasn't somehow to blame for the actress's behavior.

He skimmed several paragraphs about the drama that had taken place during filming of a romantic comedy in San Pedro, and then he found his name at the bottom of the page.

In other news: a rep for native supermodel Arianna Raquel has confirmed that the twenty-four-year-old is expecting her first child with Russian composer, Pavel Belyakova; and Prince Cameron and long-time girlfriend Allegra de Havilland were spotted dining at L'Atelier Friday evening.

He turned the page, looking for more. But that was it— barely a footnote at the very bottom of the page.

He exhaled a sigh, as surprised as he was relieved, and even more curious.

It was the curiosity that led him to track her down at her home and ask, "Why?"

Gabriella stared at him, appearing as surprised by his presence at her door at this early hour as by the inquiry.

"What are you doing here?" she demanded, completely disregarding his question to ask her own.

There was something in his tone that warned him she wasn't just surprised that he was there but…scared?

No, he was obviously misreading the situation. As she'd already proven that her pen was mightier than his sword, she had nothing to fear from him.

He shrugged. "I wanted to talk to you, but I didn't want

to have another conversation where we'd be surrounded by reporters."

"How did you know where I lived?"

"I called your editor." He'd expected a downtown address and had been surprised to find himself driving toward the outskirts of the city. He'd been even more surprised to pull up in front of a modest but well-kept two-story home on a quiet cul-de-sac.

It was a house made for a family, and it made him wonder if Gabriella had one. It wasn't unreasonable to expect that she'd married and had children at some point over the past sixteen years, even if she still looked more like a centerfold fantasy than a suburban mom.

He cut off his wandering thoughts before they could detour too far down that dangerous path, but cast a quick glance at her left hand and found that it was bare.

As bare as the long, slender legs that seemed to stretch for miles beneath the ragged hem of cutoff shorts she wore low on her hips. As bare as the sexy, curve of her shoulders peeking above the neckline of her peasant-style blouse. As bare as—

Gabriella's soft groan drew his attention back to their conversation. "You called Alli? Thanks. As if I didn't get enough of an interrogation after your appearance at the office yesterday, now you contacted her for my home address."

He cleared his throat, suddenly uncomfortably aware of her nearness, of the soft feminine scent that had always clouded his senses when he was near her. "I didn't realize that would be a problem."

"As if that would matter to you," she muttered.

"Can I come in?"

"No."

Her response—immediate and definitive—had him lifting his brows. "Do you really want to take the chance of someone spotting me standing on your doorstep?"

"If you didn't want to announce your presence to everyone on the street, you should have driven something a little more inconspicuous than an Aston Martin." But she did, reluctantly, step away from the door so that he could enter.

Of course, she didn't move any farther into the house than the foyer, and she faced him squarely, arms folded across her chest. The open-concept design allowed light to spill into the entranceway from the east-facing windows, and it surrounded Gabriella now, giving her an almost ethereal appearance. Although the dark scowl on her face spoiled the illusion somewhat.

He glanced around, appreciating how the sunny yellow walls complemented the terracotta floor. Her furniture was simple in design and neutral in color, with bold splashes of turquoise, lime and purple used as strategic accents.

"Nice place," he told her.

"Thank you," she responded stiffly. "But since I don't think you stopped by to compliment my décor, why don't you tell me why you're really here?"

"Because I can't figure you out."

"I don't know why you'd bother to try," she told him.

Her tone was dismissive, and yet, he couldn't forget the flare of awareness he'd seen in her eyes when he'd touched her arm the night before, confirming that she'd felt the same jolt that had shaken him to the core.

It had been like that between them since the first time they'd met. But he wouldn't have expected that there would be anything left of that long-ago connection, not after so many years, and especially not considering the way their relationship had ended.

He'd been young and scared of the feelings he had for her, and he'd treated her badly. He had no excuse for his behavior—and no reason to expect that she'd forgiven him, which made the absence of any mention in the gossip column of his argument with Allegra all the more puzzling.

"You could have completely skewered me in today's paper," he noted.

Her brows rose. "Because you stomped all over some poor woman's heart? That's hardly news."

"I didn't realize how badly I'd stomped on yours," he said.

She waved a hand dismissively. "Ancient history."

"Is it?" He took a step closer, watched her eyes narrow, darken.

"Yes," she said firmly.

But he could see the pulse point at the base of her jaw, and it was racing.

"I never forgot about you, Gabriella. And I don't think you forgot about me, either."

"How could I when your face is plastered on the tabloids on an almost daily basis?"

"You're not going to give me an inch, are you?"

"I've already given you a lot more than I should have." She slipped past him and reached for the handle of the door. "Now I have things to do and I'd really like you to go."

But he wasn't ready to leave. Not yet. "Who was the guy you were with last night?"

"Newsflash," she said. "I'm the reporter, you're the object of the public's curiosity. Therefore, I get to ask the questions and you get to smile and look pretty."

"Who is he?" he asked again.

She sighed. "Rafe Fulton."

The name didn't mean anything to him, but he wanted to know more than the man's identity—he wanted to know what the man meant to her. "Boyfriend?"

"Yes."

He frowned at that, but before he could say anything else, footsteps sounded overhead.

Gabriella's gaze shifted to the stairs. "You really have to go now."

He didn't particularly want to hang around to meet the boyfriend, but he was baffled by Gabriella's sudden and obvious desperation to get him out the door. Was her boyfriend the possessive type? Would he disapprove of her having a conversation with another man? Would he—Cameron's blood boiled at the thought—take out his displeasure on Gabriella?

"Gabriella—" He reached for her hand, found it icy cold.

She tugged her hand from his grasp, wrenched open the door. "Please, Cameron. Just go."

The footsteps were coming down the stairs now. Not the heavy tread he'd anticipated, but light, quick steps.

"What's for breakfast, Mom? I'm starving."

Cameron froze, his mind spinning.

Mom?

"I'm making French toast as soon as Gram gets back from the market with the eggs," Gabriella called, then hissed at him, "Please go. I don't want to explain your presence here to my daughter."

Daughter.

She wasn't trying to get rid of him for the benefit of an angry husband or possessive lover, but because she didn't want him to meet her child.

Except that the voice he'd heard didn't sound like that of a pre-schooler or even a pre-teen, but more like that of an adult.

"Mmm, I love French toast," the voice replied.

And then she stepped into view and he saw that his assessment had been right. Gabriella's daughter wasn't a little girl, but a young and stunningly beautiful woman with her mother's dark tumbling curls and distinctly feminine curves. She was dressed similarly to her mother, too, in shorts and a T-shirt, with the addition of a sling around her neck to help support the arm that was encased in a neon-yellow cast.

Except for the cast, looking at her was like looking at Gabriella sixteen years ago, and the realization nearly knocked him off of his feet.

"Whoops." The girl stopped in mid-stride when she spotted Cameron standing in the foyer beside her mother. "Sorry—I didn't realize you had company."

"It's okay," Gabriella said pointedly. "Cameron was just on his way out."

He ignored her, focusing instead on her daughter, who was eyeing him with unbridled curiosity.

As she drew nearer, he saw that the child's eyes were lighter than her mother's—more hazel than brown.

More like the color of his own eyes.

His gaze flew back to Gabriella.

She tilted her chin, as if daring him to ask. But he didn't need to ask.

In that moment, all of the pieces fell into place.

A long-ago conversation. Tear-filled eyes looking to him for answers. Desperate panic. Fierce denials. Reassurance. Relief.

He'd worked hard to forget her, to forget what they had been to one another, but she hadn't been able to forget. She'd lived with the reminder of their long-ago affair every day for the past sixteen years.

The girl standing in front of him was that reminder.

Gabriella's daughter was his daughter, too.

Mi Dios. He was a father.

As his gaze lingered on the beautiful young woman, he couldn't help but think: *Lord, help us both.*

Chapter Four

"Hey, aren't you—" Sierra's sleepy brain woke up in time to halt the impulsive flow of words. She had almost asked her mother's visitor if he was one of the royals, but thankfully she realized how ridiculous the question was before she embarrassed herself by asking it.

She shook her head but still couldn't shake the feeling that she recognized him from somewhere. "Sorry, for a minute I thought you looked...familiar."

"I am Cameron Leandres," he said, and bowed.

Sierra held back a snicker.

Was this guy for real?

Then the name clicked, and her head suddenly felt so light, she thought that she might faint.

"Then you are—ohmygod—you're *Prince* Cameron?"

"I am," he agreed, in the same casual tone.

Sierra's gaze flew to her mother, who seemed neither surprised nor impressed by this revelation.

Of course, her mother worked in the newspaper business

and she'd been covering the "Around Town" section while
Alex was on vacation. She knew everyone in the country
who was newsworthy. Obviously she would have recognized
him immediately. But that still didn't explain what the heck
the guy—the *prince*—was doing in her house. And wouldn't
Jenna just die when she heard about this?

"And you are obviously Gabriella's daughter," Prince Cameron noted.

"Sierra Vasquez," she responded automatically, wondering
if she was supposed to bow or curtsy.

She glanced at her mother again, as if for guidance, and
noticed the stiffness of her posture, the deepening of the faint
lines that bracketed her mouth. Whatever had brought this
member of the royal family to their door, it was apparent to
Sierra that Gabriella wasn't pleased by his presence.

"It's a pleasure to finally meet you, Sierra." The prince's
comment drew her attention back to him and further piqued
her curiosity.

Before she could say anything else, her mother interrupted.

"Thanks for the information, Your Highness," Gabriella
said. "I'll be sure to pass it along to Alex when he returns
from his vacation."

"There's no need for such formalities between old friends,
Gabriella," the prince chided.

Old friends?

Sierra felt her jaw drop.

She turned to her mother, noted the spots of color that rode
high on her cheeks, a telltale sign that she was either embarrassed or angry. Because she used to rub elbows with royalty?
Or because she didn't want Sierra to know that she used to
rub elbows with royalty? It made her wonder how long her
mother had known the prince—and just how close they used
to be.

Curiosity was eating away at her, but she didn't dare ask her mother those questions. At least not right now.

"What happened to your arm?"

It was the prince who spoke again, his tone was casual and friendly, as if he was unaware of the tension in the room. Or maybe he was just unconcerned about it.

She glanced cautiously at her mother, because she knew Gabriella was still angry about the events of the previous day. "Car accident."

He frowned. "You can't be old enough to drive."

"Your Highness—" Gabriella began to interject again, with obvious impatience.

"Not yet," Sierra responded to his statement. "My best friend was driving."

"I hope no one was badly injured."

She shook her head, lifted her arm slightly. "This was the worst of it."

The crunch of tires on gravel was unmistakable through the open window, evidence that her grandmother had returned from the market.

"Go help with the bags, Sierra," her mother said.

It was obvious that she was being sent out of the room so that her mother could finish her conversation with the royal visitor in private, and Sierra was itching to know why. What business had brought the prince to their home? And why was her usually composed and level-headed mother so obviously flustered by his presence?

"I think you're forgetting which one of us has the broken arm," she responded, hoping for a brief reprieve.

"Now," Gabriella snapped.

Sierra's brows lifted in response to the unexpectedly sharp tone. Her mother was definitely unnerved, and as much as she wanted to hang around and hear the rest of the conversation between them, the sound of the back door opening prompted her to do as she was told.

* * *

Gabriella breathed a silent sigh of relief when Sierra finally exited the room. She knew she'd only been granted a brief reprieve, that her daughter would have plenty of questions for her later. And she would face them later. But right now, she had to face the prince, who wasn't likely to be nearly as patient nor understanding as Sierra.

"So how old is she?" Cameron asked.

Gabriella crossed her arms over her chest. "My daughter is none of your business."

"Unless she's my daughter, too."

He'd kept his voice low, his tone even, but she couldn't resist glancing toward the doorway through which Sierra had disappeared to confirm her daughter was not within earshot. "She's not."

"How old is she?" he asked again.

She lifted her chin. "Fifteen."

"When's her birthday?"

"What gives you the right to barge in here and ask me all these questions?"

"Her birthday," he said again.

Her reply wasn't a date but a directive, and he responded to her crude words with a casual lift of his brows. His unruffled demeanor only irritated her further. Of course, he could afford to be cool—he didn't have anything to lose.

"Look, Your Highness—"

"I don't remember you ever being as hung up on my title then as you seem to be now," he mused.

She hadn't even known he had a title when they first met. If she had, she probably would never have got up the courage to even speak to him. But to her, he'd just been one of a group of college kids who regularly came into the restaurant on Friday nights. Maybe he was a little more handsome than the others, a little more charming. And he was the only one whose smile made her heart beat faster.

Even not knowing that he was royalty, she'd known that he was out of her league. Not just because he was older and more sophisticated, but because it was obvious that his family had money while her family worked for those with money. If Gabriella wanted to go to college someday, as she'd intended to do, she would have to earn the money to pay for her education. Which is how she ended up serving wood-oven pizzas and pitchers of beer to spoiled frat boys like Cameron and his buddies.

"Obviously I wasn't as discerning then as I am now," she said coolly.

"Ouch," he said, but smiled after he said it.

It was the same smile that had always made her knees a little bit weak. So easy and natural, so completely charming and utterly irresistible—at least to a seventeen-year-old girl. But she wasn't seventeen anymore and there was too much at stake to let herself to succumb once again to his considerable charms.

"Cameron." She used his name this time, and was rewarded with another smile.

"Isn't that much better, *Gabriella?*"

His pronunciation of her name was as sensual as a caress, and she felt something unwelcome and unwanted stir inside of her. "What would be much better," she told him, "would be for you to leave so that I can enjoy the rest of the day with my family."

"But we have so much to catch up on," he insisted.

Despite the casual tone, she knew the words weren't an invitation but a threat.

"Another time," she offered.

"You're only delaying the inevitable," he warned her.

She knew that might be true. But she also knew that "the partying prince" had a notoriously short attention span, and she was confident that he would soon forget about her and Sierra and this impromptu visit entirely.

"I'll be happy to meet with you at a mutually convenient date and time," she lied.

"All right," he finally said. He pulled a BlackBerry from his jacket pocket and scrolled through some data, no doubt checking his calendar. "Next Saturday afternoon. Two o'clock in front of the Naval History Museum."

"I'll have to check my schedule," she told him.

His gaze narrowed. "Next Saturday at two o'clock," he said again. "If you're not there, I'll come back here. And I won't leave until all of my questions have been answered."

"I'll be there," she agreed, because she knew that she had no choice. And because she was hoping that, at some point in the coming week, something more important would come up and he would forget.

Gabriella knew *she* wouldn't forget. Because nothing was more important to her than her daughter—and keeping the secret of Sierra's paternity.

Cameron didn't want to wait a whole week to get the answers he sought. But he wasn't entirely sure he trusted Gabriella to tell him the truth, and he knew that if he had some time, he could uncover some of the answers himself.

By Thursday afternoon, he had the most important one. As he stared at the copy of the birth certificate in his hand, his gaze focused on the date that confirmed his suspicions. Sierra Katarina Vasquez was born on June fifteenth—nine months after the weekend he and Gabriella had spent together on the northern coast. Which proved that Gabriella's beautiful fifteen-going-on-sixteen-year-old daughter was also his daughter, even if the father was listed as "unknown" on the registration of her birth.

The sight of that single word had filled him with burning fury. He was as stunned as he was incensed that she would deny the role he'd played in the creation of their child. But his anger faded almost as quickly as it had built, as snippets of a long-ago conversation filtered through his memory.

They'd had the occasional stolen moment together over the period of a few months, and then one glorious extended weekend at Cielo del Norte. When he'd dropped her off after their brief holiday was over, he'd promised that he would call her—but he never did. In fact, several weeks passed before he saw her again, before she tracked him down.

He remembered the exact moment he'd spotted her standing beside the stone archway that guarded the entrance to his campus residence. His initial surprise had been replaced by pleasure, then guilt and regret.

He wanted to go to her, to take her in his arms, to tell her how much he'd missed her. Because he had, and every time he'd thought of her, he'd felt an aching emptiness deep inside. But he'd made up his mind—he was too young to get seriously involved with any one woman—and he'd been sure that, in time, he'd get over her. So instead of going to her, he walked right past, as if he didn't even see her.

He'd thought she would take the hint, that she would turn away. But she'd raced across the field, chasing after him.

"Cameron, wait."

He couldn't pretend he hadn't heard her, so he halted, and tried to look vaguely puzzled. "Hi, uh, Gabriella, right?"

Her eyes—those beautiful, fathomless dark eyes that haunted his dreams—went wide, her face drained of all color. But then she firmed her quivering lip and lifted her chin. "Yes, it's Gabriella," she told him. "We spent a weekend together at the beach last month."

"Yeah," he nodded, as if only now remembering. As if the memories hadn't preoccupied his every waking thought and haunted his every dream since he'd said goodbye to her. "It was a good time."

She hesitated, as if she wasn't sure what else to say to him.

Then she tilted her chin another fraction and met his gaze dead-on. "I think I might be pregnant."

He couldn't see his own face, but he would have guessed that it was even whiter than hers now. He took an automatic step in retreat. "No. No way."

"I don't know for sure," she admitted, her gaze sliding away from his now. "But I thought you should know."

He shook his head. He didn't want to know. He didn't want to believe it was possible. They'd been careful. He was always careful. Except for that last morning. He'd realized that he'd run out of condoms, but he'd thought that it would be okay—he'd convinced her that it would be okay—just one time.

"When—" he managed to clear his throat, but his mind remained fuzzy "—when will you know...for sure?"

"I can pick up a test...on my way home."

He nodded and reached into his back pocket for his wallet. He didn't even count out the bills—he just pulled out all the money that he had and thrust it toward her.

She stared at the money in his hand, her eyes filling with tears.

"Just take it," he said. "In case you need anything."

She knocked the money out of his hand and turned.

"Gabriella."

"Don't worry," she said, her usually warm voice colder than he'd ever heard it before. "I don't need anything from you."

Then she'd walked away, but the tight, panicky feeling that had taken hold inside his chest didn't go away, not for a long time. But as the days turned into weeks and the weeks into months and he didn't see her or hear from her again, he'd been relieved. He'd assumed that she'd made a mistake, that she hadn't been pregnant. Now he knew otherwise.

In retrospect, he could hardly blame her for refusing to name him on her child's birth certificate. If anything, he should thank her. Because at twenty years of age, he hadn't been ready to be a parent. He didn't imagine that Gabriella had been any more ready than he, but she'd taken on the responsibility, anyway. She could have terminated her pregnancy or given the baby up for adoption, but she'd done neither. She'd given birth and raised their child on her own.

Maybe not completely alone, since it seemed that her mother had stood by her. But as far as he knew, she'd never even attempted to contact him again. Not once in the past sixteen years had she tried to get in touch with him to let him know that he was a father.

He knew he couldn't blame her for that. And yet, when he looked at the young woman who reminded him so much of Gabriella when he'd first met her so many years before, he couldn't help but resent having been excluded. Not just excluded but explicitly disavowed by that one little word: *unknown*.

And what would have been different if she'd named him on the child's birth certificate?

He instinctively winced in response to the question that echoed in the back of his head. Even now, more than sixteen years later, he couldn't pretend that everything wouldn't have spun out of control. There would have been a media circus, at the very least. As soon as anyone had seen his name on the birth certificate, the existence of his illegitimate child would have been in the headlines. And he would have responded the same way he'd responded to every scandal that he'd faced: with bald-faced, blatant denials.

He would have been instructed by his royal advisors to deny even the possibility that he was the father of Gabriella's baby. If there had been any proof that she'd spent the weekend at Cielo del Norte with him, then he'd produce a dozen more witnesses to testify to the fact that they weren't alone. She would have been portrayed as a girl of loose morals who'd gotten herself into trouble and was looking for a quick payoff by claiming he'd been with her. And if she'd tried to force the issue by demanding a paternity test, well, the Leandres name and money were more compelling than science.

Yeah, he was still mad at Gabriella Vasquez, but he figured his residual anger couldn't begin to compare to hers.

She'd had sixteen years to resent who he was and what he'd done—how was he ever going to make up for that?

Chapter Five

Gabriella never considered not showing up at the museum. She didn't dare disregard Cameron's threat about returning to her home, and if they were going to have it out about Sierra she wanted to do it somewhere else. But a full week had passed since he'd knocked on her door, and she did let herself hope that he had forgotten about this meeting, that he'd forgotten about her daughter.

Her daughter.

She repeated the words to herself, a soft whisper that couldn't be heard by anyone else, and found solace in them.

Sierra was *her* daughter. From the very beginning, Gabriella had known it would only be the two of them, that they would have to make their own way together. Cameron had made his feelings very clear and if Gabriella had let herself imagine that he might change his mind once he'd had a chance to think about the possibility of their baby, the princess royal had disabused her of that ridiculous notion.

Her own mother had been stunned when Gabriella told her

that she was pregnant. Worse, she'd been disappointed. Gabriella had seen it in her eyes, and it had shamed her. Her father had passed away when Gabriella was only ten years old, and her mother had taken on a second job after his death in order to ensure they didn't lose the house they'd always lived in. It hadn't been easy for Katarina, working two jobs and trying to be both a mother and father to her only daughter, but she'd always been there for Gabriella.

When Gabriella started showing an interest in boys, Katarina had sat down with her and talked to her about love and lust, impressing upon her the importance of respecting her body so that others would, too. Gabriella had assured her mother that she had no intentions of falling in love or falling into bed with anyone. She had plans for her life. She wanted to go to college and build a career before she even considered getting seriously involved.

And then she'd met Cameron. Prior to the first time he walked into Marconi's Restaurant, Gabriella hadn't realized that lust could race through a woman's body with such intensity, making her want with such desperation that there was no thought or reason. She'd tried to resist, but she'd been so completely inexperienced and totally unprepared to withstand his easy charm.

Or maybe she hadn't tried as hard as she should have, because even then she'd thought it was more than lust. She'd convinced herself that she was in love with him, and she'd believed him when he'd said that he was in love with her. And though her mother's warnings had echoed in the back of her mind, she didn't think there was anything wrong with two people in love making love.

It hadn't taken her long to realize she'd been duped, by her own hormones as much as his words.

But that was a lot of years ago—and she was a different woman now.

A woman who glanced at her watch for the tenth time in half as many minutes. It was almost two o'clock.

She shifted her gaze to the crowd of people who were milling around the entrance, but she didn't see Cameron anywhere. Maybe he wasn't going to show up. Maybe—

"You look like you're ready to bolt."

His voice, deep and warm and tinged with amusement, came from behind.

Gabriella whirled around, her heart pounding furiously against her ribs. "Not before two-oh-five," she assured him.

He smiled, his teeth flashing white in contrast to his tanned skin, and her knees went weak. Silently she cursed him, then cursed herself louder and harder.

"Where's your entourage of bodyguards?"

"I'm flying beneath the radar today," he told her.

She didn't see how that was possible. Even as casually dressed as he was, in well-worn jeans and a faded Cambridge University T-shirt with a battered Baltimore Orioles baseball cap on his head, there was something about him that made him stand out from the crowd. Although he dwarfed her five-feet-four-inch frame, he was probably just about six feet tall, and he was more slender than muscular. But his shoulders were broad, and he carried himself with a confidence that edged into arrogance. He was the type of man who would never go anywhere unnoticed, and the realization made Gabriella wary.

"The museum closes at three," she told him, anxious to commence and conclude this unwanted meeting.

"I didn't actually plan on going inside," he replied.

She frowned. "Then why are we here?"

"I thought we could take a walk." He offered his arm to her.

Gabriella only stared at him. "In the middle of downtown on a Saturday afternoon?"

His lips curved again, and her heart pounded.

"Are you worried about what the gossip columnists might say if we're seen together?" he teased.

"I'd think you should be the one to worry," she said, unable to deny that being seen with the prince made her uneasy. Because his baseball cap really wasn't much of a disguise.

He just shrugged. "I stopped letting rumors and innuendo bother me years ago."

She wished she could say the same thing, but the truth was, she'd always hated the idea of anyone talking behind her back, spreading gossip and lies. She only had herself to blame for the worst of it. By refusing to name the father of her baby, she'd given people reason to talk, to speculate, to sneer.

"Gabriella?"

She pushed the painful memories aside. "Where are we walking to?"

"The harbor front."

It would be even busier down by the water, but maybe that was his plan—to hide in plain sight. So she fell into step beside him, grateful that she was wearing low-heeled sandals. She'd changed her clothes four times before she'd left the house—not because she wanted to impress him but because she wanted to ensure that she didn't give that impression.

"Have you had lunch?" he asked her.

"I had a late breakfast." Truthfully, she'd barely nibbled on the omelet her mother had made for her, because her stomach was tied up in knots in anticipation of this meeting.

"We could pick up some sandwiches at The Angel and take them to the park for a picnic."

"I wouldn't have taken you for the picnicking type," she said.

"A lot changes in seventeen years."

"True enough," she agreed.

"Although you look the same," he noted. "Aside from some subtle changes. Your hair's a little shorter, your curves are a little fuller, but you still knock the breath out of me every time I see you."

"And you still have all the best lines," she retorted.

"You don't believe it's true?"

"I learned a long time ago not to believe any words that come out of your mouth."

A muscle in his jaw flexed. "I guess I can't blame you for that," he finally said.

Gabriella didn't respond. She'd promised herself that she wouldn't let him get to her, that no matter what he said or did, she would remain cool and unruffled. But after less than ten minutes in his company, she was feeling decidedly uncool and extremely ruffled.

He paused on the sidewalk outside of the café. "Proscuitto and provolone with mustard?"

She was surprised that he remembered. She'd thought it was only a coincidence that he'd chosen to stop at The Angel. She wouldn't have expected him to remember that they'd been there together once before—stopping in for provisions on the Friday afternoon before they'd stolen away for the weekend. Not only had he remembered that they'd stopped at this café, but he'd remembered what she'd ordered.

But as he'd pointed out, they weren't the same people now that they were then, and she'd changed a lot more than he could imagine. "Turkey and Swiss with mayo."

"Iced tea?"

She nodded. While he ducked inside the café, she waited outside, watching the crowd.

When Sierra was little, Gabriella would often bring her down here on weekends. They would browse through the little shops that lined the waterfront and eat sandwiches in the park, throwing their crusts to the ducks that paddled in circles around the pond. Then they'd walk a little farther, and she'd hold tightly to Sierra's hand as she said a silent thank-you to the playboy prince who lived in the fancy house that was just barely visible at the top of the hill, because he'd given her the greatest gift in the world. Then they'd go back to Lorenzo's for some lemon ice before they headed home.

She smiled at the memory, the smile slipping as she remembered that Sierra still loved to spend Saturday afternoons at the harbor front, though she usually preferred to do her shopping with Jenna and Rachel now. Gabriella had a moment of panic then, when it occurred to her that she might run into her daughter here in town. She wasn't sure what Sierra's plans were for the day, but she figured it would be just her luck to meet Cameron downtown in order to avoid him seeing Sierra again—and then running into her anyway.

"Gabriella?"

Her breath caught in her throat, but she chided herself for the instinctive reaction. The deeply, masculine voice obviously didn't belong to her daughter. As she turned to respond, the initial sense of relief was replaced by guilt and remorse when she found herself face-to-face with Rafe.

Cameron walked out of the café with a paper bag in hand and a smile on his face. He wasn't sure he could explain his good mood. He'd been furious beyond reason when he'd realized that Gabriella had given birth to his child and never bothered to tell him about his daughter, and even if he thought he understood why she'd kept that information to herself, he knew it was going to take them both some time to get past all of that history.

But he also knew that he wanted to get past it. He wanted to get to know his daughter, he wanted Sierra to know that he was her father, and he wanted a second chance with Gabriella—a first chance for the three of them to be a family.

Family. The word made his chest feel tight. At first, he'd thought his reaction was panic at the idea of being tied down to one woman and her child, but the more he thought about it, the more he'd realized what he was really feeling was a yearning. A yearning that had been stirring inside of him since he'd seen her standing in her boss's office.

Or maybe the yearning had been there for the past seventeen years. Maybe that was why he'd never had a long-term relationship with any one woman—because he'd never gotten over Gabriella. Because he couldn't help but compare every other woman he'd been with to her, and no one had ever measured up.

He shook his head, banishing the ridiculously romantic notion from his mind. He'd barely been twenty years old when they'd had their brief affair so many years ago and he hadn't been pining for her since. Truthfully, he'd hardly even let himself think about her during the intervening years. But when he'd realized she was the author of the offending "Around Town" column, he'd grasped the excuse to track her down. Yes, he'd been frustrated and angry—but he'd also been curious. He'd wanted to see her again, to find out what she'd been up to over the past seventeen years, and he was curious to know if there was anything left of the chemistry that had always sizzled between them.

There was still sizzle—and a whole lot of baggage that he never could have anticipated. But he wasn't going to worry about that today. Right now, he just wanted to spend a pleasant day with Gabriella, to learn about his daughter and convince her mother that he wanted to be part of her life again.

And maybe, if he was lucky, he might have a chance to test the potency of that chemistry. He pushed open the door, his smile fading as soon as he saw that Gabriella wasn't alone.

She was with a man, holding his hand, and the man was smiling at her in a way that left Cameron in no doubt about the fact that they'd been lovers. Maybe they still were. His fingers automatically curled into fists, and it was only when he heard the crinkle of the paper bag that he remembered it was in his hand.

"Ready, Gabriella?" His tone was deliberately casual.

She started and turned, her cheeks flushing with color. He thought she tried to tug her hand from the other man's grasp, but he held on, his smile looking a little strained now.

"Oh. That was quick," she said.

He lifted a brow, silently questioning.

"Cameron, this is Rafe Fulton. Rafe, this is Cameron."

He offered his hand, not because he felt compelled by social custom but in order to force the other man to release his hold on Gabriella, as he finally did.

"It's a pleasure," Rafe said, although the look in his eyes warned that it was anything but.

"You're American," Cameron noted, immediately picking up on the accent.

"That's right," Rafe agreed.

"New York?" he guessed.

The other man nodded. "Although I seem to spend more time traveling than I do at home these days."

"Rafe's in international banking," Gabriella explained.

"Is that why you're in Tesoro del Mar?" Cameron asked him.

"That's the reason I first visited Tesoro del Mar almost two years ago," Rafe told him, then shifted his gaze to Gabriella. "But not the reason I keep coming back."

The flush in Gabriella's cheeks deepened. "Cameron and I have some things—business—to discuss."

"Then I'll leave you to your...business," Rafe said, taking a step back. "And I'll look forward to seeing you at seven."

She nodded.

"Busy day for you today," Cameron mused, as the other man walked away.

"You picked the date and time for this meeting," she reminded him.

"I guess I did," he agreed. "I didn't realize your boyfriend would still be in town."

"Would it have made a difference if you did?" she challenged.

"No," he admitted, and began heading toward the park.

Gabriella fell into step beside him. When they found a vacant picnic table in the shade, he spread a couple of paper napkins on top before setting out their food. She opened her iced tea, took a long swallow.

Cameron took a bite of his sandwich, although his appetite had diminished. "How serious is it?"

She frowned. "What?"

"You and Rafe," he clarified. "How serious is it?"

"Is that why you wanted to see me today—to talk about my relationship with Rafe?"

Actually, that was the absolute last thing he wanted to talk about. "No—I wanted to talk about what you're planning for Sierra's birthday."

Every muscle in Gabriella's body went completely still. "What are you talking about?"

"It's June fifteenth next week," he pointed out to her. "I just assumed you'd be having a party for the big occasion."

Her cheeks paled, but her gaze never wavered. "As a matter of fact, I am."

He nodded. "A girl's sixteenth birthday is a special occasion." Then, when Gabriella remained silent, he pressed on. "It is her sixteenth birthday, isn't it?"

"Obviously you already know the answer to that question."

"Birth registrations are a matter of public record," he reminded her.

"Her age doesn't prove anything," she said.

"No," he agreed. "But I imagine a DNA test would prove plenty."

She wrapped up her untouched sandwich, her appetite obviously gone. "Do you really want to subject yourself to the sort of scandal that would entail?"

"Maybe the better question is: do you want to subject Sierra to that sort of scandal?" he challenged. "Because I'm not the one denying that she's my daughter."

She rose to her feet, facing him across the table. "You have no right—"

"I think the courts would agree that I have plenty of rights," he assured her.

Her eyes filled with tears. "You bastard."

"Actually, *my* parents were legally married when I was conceived."

"Which just goes to prove that having both a father and a mother isn't a guarantee of anything," she snapped.

"You never did pull your punches," he mused.

She stormed away. He abandoned the remnants of their lunch to follow her into a stand of trees.

"What do you want from me?"

He wasn't sure there was a simple answer to that question, so he only said, "I want a chance to know my child."

"Why?"

"Because she's my child."

Gabriella didn't waste any more breath trying to deny it. When she spoke again, it was only to say, "She doesn't know you're her father."

"Maybe it's time that she did," he told her.

Her gaze flew to his—her dark eyes filled with anger and frustration. "What gives you the right, after sixteen years, to make that decision?"

"How about the fact that, for sixteen years, I didn't know I had a child?"

"You didn't want to know," she reminded him.

He couldn't deny that was true, at least in the beginning. But the situation was different now, and he had no intention of continuing to deny his relationship to Sierra. "When is her party?"

"You're not invited."

"That wasn't what I asked," he said mildly.

She huffed out a breath. "Saturday night. Eight o'clock. And you're not invited."

"Where?"

"Cameron—"

"At your house," he guessed.

"Yes," she admitted. "It's a surprise and you're not invited."

"Do you really think you can keep me away?"

"I think you should be able to see the potential for disaster if you show up. It only took Sierra a few minutes to figure out who you are and once her friends realize you're royalty, well, there will be pictures of you all over the internet before the birthday candles are even lit."

"I might be more inclined to appreciate your concern if you weren't responsible for so much of my bad press of late."

"Honestly, I don't care what kind of photos or videos the kids snap of you. I *do* care how your presence at the party might impact Sierra. What possible explanation could you give for being there?"

"Other than the truth, you mean?"

She glared at him. "Other than that."

"I'll be your date," he suddenly decided.

"I don't think so."

"I'm sure you could accept that more easily than explaining to all of the guests that I'm the birthday girl's father."

She folded her arms across her chest. "And how am I supposed to explain to my daughter that I'm dating someone other than my fiancé?"

He frowned at that. "You and Rafe are engaged?"

"Yes," she told him, but her defiant gaze flickered away.

"Then why aren't you wearing his ring?" he demanded.

She blinked, as if startled by the question. "It's, uh, it's a little big, so I've decided not to wear it until I've had a chance to get it adjusted."

"Really?" He considered her explanation for a moment, then shook his head. "If he was serious enough to buy a ring, he'd make sure it was the right size so he could slide it on your finger as soon as you said 'yes.'"

She didn't respond.

"Or maybe that's the real reason you're not wearing it," he continued. "Because you haven't said 'yes.'"

"My relationship with Rafe isn't any of your business."

"It is when you keep using it as a roadblock between us."

"There is no 'us,'" she said again.

He hadn't seen her in more than sixteen years, so her statement was hardly unreasonable. And yet, something about her adamant tone irked him, made him want to prove differently. Unable to think of any words that might convince her, he kissed her instead.

Chapter Six

Gabriella had all kinds of reasons for not ever wanting to see Cameron Leandres again, and only one for acceding to his request: Sierra. She'd thought—desperately hoped—that she might convince the prince that he had no reason to believe her daughter was also his. She hadn't let herself think of her own feelings. Or maybe she hadn't believed that she could have any feelings for the man who had broken her heart so many years before. But the moment his lips touched hers, she knew that she'd made a very dangerous miscalculation.

Because in that first whisper-soft brush of his mouth against hers, she was catapulted back in time. It was as if everything she was feeling was new and unfamiliar and all-encompassing. She hadn't just been a virgin when she'd met Cameron, but an innocent in far more ways than she'd realized—completely unprepared for the depth and breadth of the emotions and desires that he brought to life within her. But she'd been an avid pupil of his experienced seduction, an eager participant in their lovemaking.

This was only a kiss—and should have been simple enough for Gabriella to resist. But she had never been able to resist Cameron. She'd known from the beginning that a relationship between them could never work out—his family was blue-blood, hers was blue-collar—but she'd somehow got caught up in the romantic fantasy, anyway. She'd let herself hope and dream, and she'd had her heart shattered.

Afterward, she'd convinced herself that what she'd felt with him hadn't been all that she'd remembered. That it was only an unfortunate combination of teenage hormones and inexperience that had made her behave so recklessly and impulsively. She'd found some solace in that, and a certain amount of relief that she'd never felt so out-of-control with any other man. Not even the man who'd asked her to marry him.

But suddenly, hidden in the shadows of the trees, she was feeling it all again. The same desperate, burning need; the same fiery, raging desire. And she was no more prepared for the feelings now than she'd been when she was seventeen. As his lips moved over hers, demanding rather than coaxing now, she responded, giving him all that he wanted, showing him all that she wanted. His fingers tangled in her hair and he tipped her head farther back, deepening the kiss. Her lips parted, their tongues met, desires tangled.

He nibbled on her bottom lip, murmured some words that her swirling mind couldn't begin to decipher. Then his hand slid up to her breast, his thumb brushing over the crest, and she whimpered low in her throat.

She knew this was wrong—being here with him, kissing him, wanting him. But she couldn't seem to help herself. She couldn't stop her heart from pounding, her blood from pulsing, or her body from yearning. But she could hate him for it. And she did.

She pulled away, her eyes burning with tears that she refused to shed. Not for this man. Not ever again.

He cupped her chin, forced her to meet his gaze. "You're not going to marry that American."

"Whether or not I marry Rafe has nothing to do with you."

"If you were really in love with him, you wouldn't have kissed me back."

"Kissing you only proved to me how lucky I am to have Rafe," she retorted.

He stepped closer, his gaze dark and foreboding. "You should be careful about throwing his name in my face," he warned. "Especially when your lips are still warm from mine."

She tilted her chin, met his stare evenly. "Don't worry. It won't happen again."

"Don't make promises you can't keep," he warned her. "But putting that aside for now, it is you who has a decision to make."

"What decision is that?" she asked warily.

"Whether to uninvite your American friend to Sierra's birthday party so that I can be your date—or to introduce me to our daughter as her father."

Of course, they both knew what her decision would be. She'd spent the better part of sixteen years protecting Sierra from the publicity that would be generated by the truth of her paternity, and she had no intention of subjecting her daughter to the headlines now. "I guess I'll see you next Saturday at eight."

Cameron understood why Gabriella was concerned about the media discovering the truth about Sierra's paternity. While being a royal entitled one to many perks, the status also came with restrictions—one of which was the inability to talk about personal issues without worry that confessions would end up on the front page of the morning newspaper. Experience had taught Cameron that the only people he could trust to keep his secrets were his family, so when he and Gabriella parted ways after their lunch in the park, he drove toward his brother's house in the exclusive gated community of Verde Colinas.

Michael and his wife had lived there happily for thirteen years, and when Samantha died almost two years earlier, Cameron had expected that his brother would want to move out of the home they'd shared together. But Michael had no intention of going anywhere, and only those family and close friends who had known him when Samantha was alive knew how much of a toll her death had taken on him. Their sister, Marissa, had contacted Cameron several times over the past few months, hoping that he would have some advice or insights on how to reach Michael, to make him see that he still had family who cared about him and—most importantly—a daughter who needed him.

Their efforts had been unsuccessful, but Marissa remained optimistic. "I'm sure he just needs time," she'd said to Cameron during a recent conversation. "Samantha was such a huge part of his life for so many years—it can't be easy to get over that kind of loss."

Cameron wouldn't know. He didn't think he'd ever been all the way in love. In fact, the closest he'd ever come had probably been with Gabriella, and that was too many years ago to even count. Since then, he'd mostly avoided personal entanglements, and—Allegra's dashed hopes aside—most of the women he dated knew he wasn't looking for anything serious or long-term.

He'd had more than a few women claim to be in love with him over the years, but he knew that what they really loved was being with a prince. Too often the words had been followed by a request—"I love you and I miss you so much when you're gone. Maybe this time I could go to Australia/Bermuda/China with you." Or a demand—"If you loved me, you would get me tickets to the concert/talk to someone about that parking infraction/buy me that condo at the waterfront."

That was a favorite of his mother's tricks—playing the affection/demand card to get what she wanted, and it had taught Cameron that everyone wanted something from him.

Everyone except his sister, he realized, when Marissa answered the door. She was the one person who always gave so much more than she ever asked for. She led him into the kitchen now and immediately began to make a pot of coffee.

"Michael's not here?" he guessed.

She shook her head. "He's at the office."

He heard music coming from the other room, and he peeked around the corner to see his twenty-one-month-old niece spinning in circles to the music.

"On a Saturday?" he responded to Marissa's statement about his brother's whereabouts.

"He said something about a big project outline he had to finish," she explained.

"And you're here watching Riley again," he guessed.

"The nanny only works until six and not at all on weekends, so I've been helping out when I can," she admitted.

As if on cue, the little girl raced into the room. She halted when she saw Cameron, then smiled shyly before she lifted her arms to her aunt.

Marissa scooped her up with one arm and an ease that revealed she'd done the same thing countless times before.

"How often is that?" he asked.

His sister shifted the child to her other hip, and shifted her gaze away from his.

"Marissa?" he prompted.

"I've moved into the spare room downstairs," she admitted.

"You've moved in?"

She shrugged. "It got me out of Mother's house."

"I'm sure she had something to say about this arrangement," he noted dryly. The princess royal always had an opinion, especially when it came to her children.

"I don't even know if she's realized I'm gone," Marissa told him.

He frowned but didn't argue her claim. It was a well-known fact that Elena paid scant attention to her only daughter, choosing to focus her energies and ambitions on her two sons. Both he and Michael had disappointed her in that regard, making Cameron wonder if their mother might have made a mistake in disregarding her daughter's potential. Except that his sister was too pure of mind and soft of heart to fall in with their mother's machinations, which was one of the reasons that he'd come to her now. Because she was also too loyal and sweet to judge the brother who had made more mistakes than he cared to admit.

"She hasn't come around here in a while," Marissa continued, rubbing the baby's back. "I think she's finally realized that Michael may never forgive her."

"For what now?" Cameron asked.

"For convincing Samantha to get pregnant—in order to ensure the continuation of the Leandres line."

And it was as a result of complications that arose during childbirth that Samantha had lost her life.

"Then, when the baby was born, Mother didn't want to have anything to do with her."

"Because she was a girl," he guessed, pouring himself a cup of the freshly brewed coffee.

She nodded.

"Then I guess there's no reason that I should feel compelled to share my news."

"What's your news?"

"That she has another granddaughter."

Marissa gaped at him. "You're a daddy?"

He smiled as he nodded. "I can't imagine her calling me

'daddy,' though, considering that she's almost sixteen years old."

His sister sank into a chair. "A teenager."

He nodded again.

"I can't believe it."

"I'm still getting used to the idea myself," he admitted.

"You didn't know?"

"Not until a few days ago."

"Are you...sure?" she asked hesitantly.

"That she's mine, you mean?"

Now it was Marissa's turn to nod.

"Yeah, I'm sure. If for no other reason than that Gabriella tried so hard to deny it."

"I'm assuming Gabriella is the mother."

"She is," he confirmed. "Gabriella Vasquez."

"Oh, this just keeps getting better and better," Marissa said, amusement evident in her tone. "And it certainly explains why the columnist always seemed to have a chip on her shoulder where you were concerned."

"Don't tell me you read that drivel."

His sister's chin went up. "It's not drivel, it's interesting. And while she strikes me as a very savvy lady, I do have to wonder how and where the two of you ever hooked up."

"She was a waitress at Marconi's," he admitted. "And from the first moment I laid eyes on her, I was seriously smitten."

Marissa's brows rose. "How did I not know any of this?"

"You were away at school at the time, and we weren't together for very long," Cameron explained.

"Long enough, obviously," she remarked dryly.

He couldn't disagree with that.

"So what went wrong? What did you do that prevented Gabriella from telling you that she was pregnant? Because I know that you have your faults, but I also know that you wouldn't walk away from your responsibilities."

He stared into the mug of coffee cradled between his hands

and wondered what he'd ever done to deserve her loyalty. "I think she tried to tell me, but I didn't want to hear it. I was young and scared and I'd just been subjected to another of our mother's endless lectures about the duties and responsibilities of being royal and—"

"And you let her come between you and the only woman you'd ever loved," Marissa told him.

He frowned. "I was twenty years old. What did I know about love?"

"You probably knew more then than you do now—because you've spent the past sixteen years trying to forget about her."

"You're such a hopeless romantic, Mar."

"Because I can believe in love even though I've never experienced it myself?" she challenged.

"Because you believe that the chemistry that draws a man and a woman together is based on elusive emotion when the reality is that the male-female attraction is founded on lust rather than love."

"Lust flares hot and bright and burns out quickly," she told him. "Love endures."

"And you know this how?"

"It's obvious—at least to me—that you still have feelings for Gabriella Vasquez, even after all this time. The only question now, big brother, is what do you intend to do about those feelings?"

It was a question that Cameron couldn't begin to answer.

When Gabriella returned home, it was to an empty house. Not wanting to think about Cameron or Rafe or the million things she had to do before Sierra's birthday party the following weekend, she decided to spend some time working on her column instead.

Unfortunately, the first letter she opened proved that escape from her own problems was impossible.

Dear Gabby,

My boyfriend of two years recently asked me to marry him and although I'm now wearing his ring, I'm not sure that I'm ready to make that kind of lifelong commitment. I said "yes" when he proposed because I do love him and because I figured a long engagement would give us both the time we needed to be sure that we want to be together forever.

But he insists that he doesn't want to wait, that he wants to start our life together right now. He says that if I really love him, I'll marry him.

I do love him, but I'm only twenty-one. He insists that he's ready to settle down and has warned that if I'm not ready to start a life with him, he'll find someone else who is.

Should I set a date or bide my time?

Signed,

Muddled about Marriage

The email address from which the letter had been sent clearly identified "Muddled" as the VP of a local telecommunications company, a title that carried more prestige than power and was granted to her upon graduation from college by the president—her father—only a few months before his death. Now, less than a year later, her twenty-first birthday celebration had been big news because it meant unrestricted access to her trust fund.

Gabriella considered for a moment, wondering if this additional information would impact the advice she intended to give "Muddled," and decided that it would not. Even if the letter writer wasn't an heiress and her fiancé wasn't so obviously a fortune-hunter, her response would be the same: ditch the jerk *now* before you're stuck with him forever.

Of course, she was a little more subtle in her formal response.

Dear Muddled,

If you're not sure that you're ready to make a lifelong commitment, then you're definitely not ready and your fiancé shouldn't be pressuring you and he definitely shouldn't be issuing ultimatums.

If he loves you, he will wait, and if he finds someone else while he's waiting, then he obviously isn't as committed to you as he claims to be—and if that's the case, it's much better to find out before you speak the vows that will tie you together.

If he continues to pressure you, then you should set a date—to move on with your life without him. Because if you let him propel you down the aisle before you're sure that it's what you want, you'll find yourself standing at the altar and kissing a frog!

Good luck,

Gabby

Gabriella re-read the letter and her response, then clicked to save it on her computer. She felt comfortable with the advice she was giving to the young woman, but as she lifted her gaze to glance at the clock above her desk, the light blue box on the shelf caught her eye and she sighed.

"Muddled" was right to be concerned—she was young, she'd barely had a chance to experience life and shouldn't be rushing to tie herself down—especially when she had reason to suspect her boyfriend's motivations. Gabriella had no similar excuse.

She was almost thirty-four years old and she'd known Rafe for two years. He was handsome, charming, intelligent, successful and wealthy, and she'd been attracted to him from the beginning. So why was she hesitating?

She lifted the box down from the shelf and opened the lid, blinking at the flash of white fire that seemed to erupt from within. The ring was truly dazzling—a three-carat heart-shaped diamond in a platinum bezel setting—and she was sure it had cost Rafe a small fortune.

He hadn't pressured her, but she knew that her almost-fiancé had believed it was only a matter of time until she took the ring out of the box and put it on her finger. Gabriella wasn't so certain.

What if I'm never ready?

But, of course, she hadn't actually spoken those words aloud. She hadn't dared ask the question that might have alerted him to the reality of her emotional scars. She'd been too afraid that he would walk away from her forever. And though she wouldn't blame him if he did, she wasn't ready to lose him. She couldn't commit to spending the rest of her life with him, but she didn't want to live her life without him, either. She didn't want to be alone.

She carefully—almost cautiously—took the ring out of the box and slipped it onto the third finger of her left hand. It fit perfectly, as Cameron had correctly assumed it would, but it felt heavy. Part of the sensation was a direct result of the size of the rock, but she knew that it felt a lot heavier than it really was, that it was the weight of expectations that felt so cumbersome when she put the diamond on her finger. With a sigh of sincere regret, she put the ring back in the box.

She'd hoped that she could wear it someday, but she knew now that it would never happen. She'd thought her heart was sufficiently mended that she could fall in love again, but as wonderful as Rafe was, something had always held her back. After the kiss she'd shared with Cameron in the park, she knew that it wasn't something but some*one*. And she knew that she would have to tell Rafe the truth about her feelings.

She was still at her computer, staring unseeingly at another reader letter, when the doorbell rang. She automatically rose to respond to the summons, surprised to find Rafe on the step.

"It can't be seven o'clock already," she said, wondering how she could have lost track of so much time.

"It's not," he admitted. "But I decided I couldn't wait until then to see you."

She moved away from the door so that he could enter. He stepped into the entranceway, but didn't go any farther.

"Something's wrong," she guessed.

"I've decided to go back to New York. Tonight."

Her throat was suddenly tight and dry, so that she had to swallow before she could ask, "Why?"

"Because as long as you're still hung up on Sierra's father, you're never going to be able to make a commitment to me."

She dropped her gaze, felt her cheeks flush, but she had to ask, "How did you know he's Sierra's father?"

"It wasn't anything obvious," he assured her. "It certainly isn't as if she looks like him—it was more the way he was looking at you. And the way he looked at me when he saw me with you, like he wanted to tear me apart for daring to touch his woman."

She shook her head. "It isn't like that. We're not...involved."

His smile was wry. "I can't tell if you're really that naive or if you think I am."

"We're not," she insisted. "Until last week, I hadn't even seen him in more than sixteen years."

Rafe looked unconvinced. "I always figured you were still harboring feelings for the man who'd fathered your daughter, but I also figured, with time, you'd get over him. Of course, I never expected that he would turn out to be a prince."

"What difference does that make?"

"Maybe none," he allowed. "Maybe your feelings have nothing to do with his title and everything to do with the fact that he was the first man you ever loved—the man you still love."

She shook her head again, refusing to acknowledge that it might be true, refusing to even consider that she might be so foolish as to harbor any feelings for a man who had proven years ago that he'd never really cared about her.

But Rafe only lifted a hand and laid his palm against her cheek. She closed her eyes, savoring the warmth of his touch, and wishing she could feel more.

"I can't make you love me," he said, as if reading her thoughts. "And I can't accept any less." Then he dipped his head and kissed her softly. "Goodbye, Gabriella."

She watched him drive away, as she had so many times before, but this time, she knew that it truly was goodbye.

Chapter Seven

The morning of Sierra's sixteenth birthday was sunny and bright, and the only thing that put a damper on her spirits was the cast that still weighed heavily on her broken arm.

Her grandmother brought a tray to her bedroom, preserving the "breakfast in bed" tradition that had been a birthday ritual in the Vasquez household for as long as Sierra could remember.

She sniffed the air, hummed her approval. "Fresh chocolate chip waffles?"

"They are your favorite," Katarina said, settling the tray across her granddaughter's lap.

Sierra took in the glass of orange juice, the bowl of fresh fruit with a dollop of yogurt, the small pitcher of warm syrup, the plate of waffles—already cut up, in deference to her injury—and the vase with a single white rose, and smiled. "You spoil me."

"That's what *abuelas* are supposed to do."

"If I eat all of this, I won't fit into the dress I was planning to wear tonight," Sierra warned, spearing a piece of waffle with her fork.

"Then you should have bought a bigger size," Katarina said, with only the slightest hint of disapproval in her tone. Though they didn't often battle over Sierra's wardrobe, the teen knew that her grandmother didn't favor the figure-hugging fashions that were currently in style.

"What if I share my waffles with you instead?"

"You're just like your mother at your age—with an answer for everything," Katarina said, shaking her head in what Sierra took to be a combination of exasperation and affection.

"Where is Mom?" Sierra asked, popping another piece of waffle into her mouth.

"Right here," Gabriella said, carrying an enormous vase overflowing with tropical blooms. She set the flowers on the table beside the bed and leaned over to kiss Sierra's cheek. "Happy Sweet Sixteen."

"Where did those come from?" Sierra asked.

"Rafe sent them," Gabriella told her.

"Is he coming for dinner with us tonight?" she asked.

Her mother and grandmother exchanged a look, and then Gabriella shook her head. "Rafe went back to New York."

"Oh." Although Sierra couldn't deny her disappointment, she was more concerned about her mother's apparent reluctance to share the information. "Is everything okay with you two?"

"Yes. No." Gabriella sighed, then lowered herself onto the edge of the mattress as Katarina hustled away on the pretext of cleaning up the kitchen. "Rafe and I... We're not seeing each other anymore."

Sierra felt her jaw drop open. "But...why?"

"He wanted more of a commitment from me than I was ready to make."

Though her tone was casual, Sierra knew that her mother's

feelings for the American were not, and that knowledge only baffled her more. "You're not going to marry him?"

Gabriella shook her head.

Sierra narrowed her gaze. "Is it because of Prince Cameron?"

Her mother's head shot up, her eyes went wide. "Why would you ask something like that?"

"Because you've been acting kind of weird ever since that day he showed up here."

Her mother hesitated, just long enough to convince Sierra that her suspicions weren't unfounded.

"I was just surprised to see him after such a very long time," Gabriella said. "But even before Cameron showed up, I knew I couldn't marry Rafe."

"So I guess that means we won't be going to New York City, either," Sierra said, aware that she sounded like a spoiled child.

"There's no reason we can't go for a visit on our own sometime," Gabriella promised her. "If we save our pennies."

Sierra sipped her juice and tried not to resent the fact that they wouldn't have had to worry about pennies if her mother had decided to marry Rafe. He could have flown them all to New York City—and anywhere else they wanted to go—on his company's private jet.

"So it's just you and me and Grandma tonight," Sierra clarified. She knew her mother had planned a party and that all of her friends would be at the house later, but she played along, not wanting to ruin the surprise.

Gabriella fussed with the flower arrangement, repositioning an enormous pink lily. "And Prince Cameron might stop by later."

Sierra nearly choked on a piece of pineapple. "Why?"

"To wish you a happy birthday," Gabriella said.

But Sierra suspected that the real answer wasn't nearly as simple as her mother wanted her to believe.

* * *

Gabriella hated being less than completely honest with Sierra, but she wasn't nearly ready for the life she'd built with her daughter to come crashing down around them, and she hated knowing that that was exactly what would happen when the truth about Sierra's paternity came to light.

And she knew that it would eventually come to light. Now that Cameron had figured it out, there would be no stopping it. And as concerned as Gabriella was about her daughter's potential response to the news, she had more reasons than that to worry. Because when Sierra was only a baby, she'd struck a deal, and she knew now that it was only a matter of time before the promise she'd made would be broken. And though the bargain might be destroyed through no fault of her own, she knew there would be repercussions.

A knock at the door startled her from her reverie.

She set down the knife she'd been using to chop veggies and made her way to the door, expecting Beth or Rachel, who had volunteered to come by to help set up for the party while Jenna kept Sierra occupied and away from the house. She wasn't expecting Cameron, and her heart gave a traitorous thump against her ribs when she opened the door and found him standing there.

"You're about five hours early," she told him.

"I know," he admitted, unfazed by her lack of welcome. "But I wanted to show you what I picked out for Sierra before I gave it to her tonight."

"You didn't have to get her a gift," Gabriella protested.

"I could hardly come empty-handed to a sweet sixteen birthday party."

"And yet, your hands are empty," she noted.

"It's an expression," he chided. "The gift is parked across the street."

Parked?

Gabriella's stomach twisted into painful knots as she looked up and spotted the shiny yellow sports car with an enormous pink bow on its roof.

"You've got to be kidding."

He frowned. "What's wrong?"

"What's wrong?" she echoed, incredulous. "Do you really think that's an appropriate gift?"

"I can exchange it for another color, if she doesn't like it. Of course, I don't know what she likes and doesn't like, but I noticed that her cast was yellow and thought she might be fond of the color."

"It's not the color—it's that it's a car," she said, incensed. "You can't give her a car."

"Why not?"

She stared at him, stunned by his obvious lack of comprehension. "Firstly, because she just turned sixteen and doesn't even have her driver's license yet. Secondly, because it's far too extravagant a gift from someone who is supposedly only here as my date."

He frowned. "Considering that I've missed sixteen years of birthdays, I don't think it's extravagant at all."

"Of course you wouldn't," she muttered.

"Every teenager wants a car," he pointed out reasonably.

"That doesn't mean they should have one."

"Why are you being obstinate about this?"

"Maybe because I'm her mother and I know that Sierra isn't old enough or responsible enough for a car of her own, and even if she was, I wouldn't let her drive around in a brand-new lemon-yellow sports car."

"So it's the specific kind of vehicle and not the car itself that you have a problem with?"

She shook her head. "Take it back."

He frowned. "And get her what instead?"

"A gift certificate for the movies. A basket of bath products. A teddy bear." She ticked the suggestions off on her fingertips.

He lifted his brows. "A teddy bear?"

"Something casual and inexpensive," she explained.

"I think she'd rather have the car."

"She'd love the car," Gabriella admitted. "Just as she'd love an unlimited shopping allowance or a trip to New York City, but she doesn't expect to have either of those things handed to her, either."

Cameron frowned. "Why would she want to go to New York City? Did your American friend offer to take her there?"

She sighed. "This isn't about Rafe—it's about you getting that car away from here before Sierra gets home."

"All right," he finally agreed, but when he looked over at the car again, regret was clearly etched in his features. "It's too bad, though. She's a beautiful vehicle and drives like a dream."

"What is a dream to you would be a nightmare to me, because I'd worry every time she drove away from the house," she told him.

"I'm sure you've had enough worries, raising Sierra on your own for sixteen years, and it certainly wasn't my intention to add to that."

She was surprised by the sincerity in his tone, touched by his understanding. "I haven't been entirely on my own," she reminded him. "I've had my mother to help out along the way."

"And now you have me."

"Cameron—"

He touched his fingers to her lips, silencing her protest. "I realize that we have a lot of details still to work out, but I want you to know that I'm not going to walk away this time. Not from Sierra, and not from you."

Somehow his words left her feeling more apprehensive than reassured.

*   *   *

Cameron decided to go with the teddy bear. Of the options Gabriella had enumerated, it seemed the best choice. Or so he thought, until he began to search and realized there were many different sizes, colors and styles of bears. In the end, he found what he was looking for in a specialty children's shop down at the waterfront.

When he returned to the house, just before nine o'clock, the party was in full swing. Gabriella had suggested that it would be simpler if he came after the "surprise" part so he didn't have to explain to anyone who he was or answer too many questions about why he was there. As it turned out, most of Sierra's friends either didn't recognize him or didn't care, because they barely paid any attention to him when he arrived. Music was pumping out of speakers and many of the party guests were crowded together on the small patio and moving to the music while others danced happily on the lawn. To be relatively unobtrusive in a crowd was a new experience, but he didn't mind. It allowed him to hover in the background and observe Sierra.

His daughter.

He watched her move through the crowd, stopping now and again to talk and laugh with her friends, or swaying her hips and tossing her head in tune with the music. For some reason, he found himself thinking of Riley—his brother's daughter, and the way she'd spun in circles watching the skirt of her dress twirl around her legs. And suddenly he was thinking about how much time he'd missed with his own child—who was already a woman.

He wondered what she'd looked like as a baby, whether he would have recognized any parts of himself in her features. Had she been a shy toddler who hid behind her mother's legs whenever a stranger spoke to her, or one of those precocious children who was happy to make friends with everyone who crossed her path? And the more he thought about all these things that he didn't know, the angrier he got.

He heard a soft, familiar laugh and glanced over as Gabriella stepped onto the porch, a glass of wine in each hand. It was her fault. As far as he was concerned, she was the one who had deprived him of the opportunity to share in all of Sierra's milestones and moments—and not just the big events, like her first day of school and special occasions, but all of the ordinary days in between.

He wanted to hate her. He *should* hate her. She was the reason he didn't know the beautiful girl on the dance floor who was his daughter. But just looking at Gabriella—in a halter-style top that left her tanned shoulders bare and a long swirling skirt with painted toes peeking out beneath—he felt a complicated mix of emotions, none of which was hate.

She was somehow even sexier now than she'd been when they first met, and despite their history and secrets, he was just as attracted to her now as he'd been back then.

Lust flares hot and bright and burns out quickly. Love endures.

He pushed the echo of his sister's words from his mind. He was *not* in love with Gabriella. Maybe he didn't hate her, but he didn't forgive her, either. Which only made it all the more difficult to figure out how the hell he was supposed to deal with her.

He watched her approach. Her bare feet made no sound on the deck, but there was a rope of gold chain slung low on her hips that jangled with every step she took. She'd always had an innate sensuality that stirred his blood, and his response was immediate and intense.

She was smiling, as if she was truly happy to see him. He knew she was only playing her part, giving him an excuse for being there. And while part of him wanted to curse her for the fact that he needed an excuse, a bigger part was content to simply enjoy looking at her.

As his gaze zeroed in on her mouth, he couldn't help but remember the day of their picnic in the park. Kissing her in the shadows of the trees. The taste of her sweet lips, the press of her soft body against his, the passion of her response. As he pushed the memories to the back of his mind, he couldn't help but wonder if his feelings for Gabriella had always been more complicated than he'd wanted to acknowledge.

She offered him one of the glasses she carried. "It's a cabernet. Not up to your usual standards, I'm sure, but decent."

He took the glass, sipped, and nodded in agreement with her assessment. "Was she surprised?"

Gabriella's lips curved. "She pretended to be. But more importantly, she's with her family and friends and having fun."

"Not all of her family," he noted.

She sighed. "Tell me again why I let you come."

"Because you knew you couldn't keep me away."

"I guess that would explain it." She nudged him toward a long table that was laden down with enormous platters of food. There were hot and cold hors d'oeuvres, crudités and dips, little sandwiches and quiches, mini-pastries and assorted sweets, and an enormous bowl of punch. "But since you're here, you might as well have something to eat."

He picked up a plate. "It's quite a spread you've put out."

"Teenagers—even teenage girls—like to eat, and my mother likes to fuss."

"She did all of this?"

"Most of it," Gabriella admitted. "I was assigned a few simple tasks—chopping vegetables, cutting sandwiches— basically, things that I couldn't screw up too badly."

"You're not much of a cook?"

She shook her head. "That domestic talent seems to have skipped my generation. Sierra, on the other hand, is a natural in the kitchen."

Just one more thing that he hadn't known. But before he

could comment on it, someone lowered the volume on the music to announce that it was time for Sierra to open her gifts. Gabriella tugged on his arm, drawing him closer to the crowd that had gathered around the birthday girl.

The presents had been set on another table, and he'd added his to the pile when he'd arrived. Sierra took her time opening each one, exclaiming over every item and sincerely thanking the individual giver. There were CDs and DVDs and books and clothes, and she seemed genuinely delighted with each item. And yet, when she picked up the glossy pink bag that contained his gift, Cameron felt his palms go damp and his breath catch in his throat.

She read the card, then her eyes searched for him in the crowd. He'd signed it simply "Cameron" and she took the cue, introducing him to the gathering as a friend of her mother's without mention of his title. Then she pulled the tissue out of the bag and reached inside, making a soft sound of surprised pleasure when she found the bear. She held it to her breast, her eyes sparkling and her lips curving wide, and Cameron's heart started to beat again.

Gabriella watched her daughter cuddle the teddy bear that Cameron had given to her, Sierra's first gift from her father, and her heart simply melted.

It wasn't the casual, inexpensive gift that Gabriella had suggested. Even from a distance, she could see the tag on the left ear that identified the bear as a Steiff. But Sierra's appreciation of the gift had nothing to do with its price tag and everything to do with her pleasure at being able to add the gorgeous blond mohair bear to her collection.

"Good call," she murmured to Cameron.

"It was your idea," he reminded her.

"And thank you—for backing down on the car."

He shrugged. "You know her better than I do, obviously,

and if you say she isn't ready, then I'll respect your judgment on that."

"It's not the only thing she isn't ready for," she warned.

"You're worried about her learning the truth about who I am," he guessed.

She nodded.

"When do you think she will be ready?" He was trying to be patient, but he'd already lost sixteen years with his daughter and he didn't intend to lose any more.

"I don't know," she admitted. "I'm just asking you to give her a chance to get to know you first, before you turn her whole world upside down."

"Is it really Sierra's world that you're worried about—or your own?"

She heard the challenge in his voice, and thought she understood. Finding out that he'd fathered a child so many years ago had obviously affected him, but he still didn't—couldn't—know what it meant to truly be a parent. He couldn't know that Sierra's world and her world were one and the same, that when Sierra hurt, Gabriella hurt right along with her.

"In a lot of ways, Sierra is very mature for her age. So much so that I sometimes forget that she's only sixteen, that her heart is still vulnerable. And while I have no doubt there's a part of her that still yearns for a father as much as she did when she was ten, she's not going to be as unquestioning or accepting of your sudden appearance in her life as she would have been back then."

"Then maybe you should have found me six years ago," he retorted. "Better yet, sixteen years ago."

"Because you would have been thrilled to learn that you were a father," she said, not even trying to mask her sarcasm.

"No," he admitted. "But at least I would have known."

"I tried to tell you," she reminded him. She didn't want to talk about what was still a painful memory for her, but she couldn't let him continue to play the injured party without bearing any responsibility for the choices they'd both made. "You didn't even know who I was."

He winced. "That's not true—"

"Don't," she said, her voice sharp. "I'd heard the rumors. I knew that you were just looking for a good time. But I let myself believe that we had something special, that you really cared about me. Of course, you made sure I believed it— because you knew it was the only way you would get me into bed."

"I *did* care about you, dammit."

She turned away, refusing to listen to his lies, refusing to acknowledge that there was still a tiny part of her heart that wanted to believe him. "I'm going to get the cake."

Chapter Eight

Cameron followed her into the house.

He wasn't ready to let their conversation drop, but he realized that their daughter's birthday party might not be the best time or place to continue it. He wanted answers. There was so much he wanted to know, but he also knew that he had to be prepared to face Gabriella's questions—and Sierra's, too—to explain the things he'd said and done so many years ago, to accept responsibility for his own actions.

For now, he only watched as Gabriella carefully arranged sixteen pink candles around the elaborately scrolled letters that spelled out "Happy Sweet Sixteen, Sierra."

"More of your mother's work?" he asked.

Gabriella nodded.

"It's beautiful."

"Wait until you taste it," she told him. "Dominic Donatella has been trying to wrangle her buttercream icing recipe out of her for more than twenty years."

"Donatella—as in Donatella's Bakery?"

She nodded again, but her eyes—still focused on the cake—filled with tears.

"Gabriella?"

"Sorry, birthdays always make me a little nostalgic, and I can't believe it's her sixteenth already." She blew out a soft breath. "When she was little, she used to think really hard about her wish, then she'd squeeze her eyes shut and blow with all of her might. She was so serious about her wishes, so certain she could make them come true."

"Do you know what kinds of things she wished for?"

"A lot of the usual things—dolls and puppies and ponies. And then, the year she turned ten, she told me that what she really wanted, more than anything in the world, was to be a princess."

She made a show of counting the candles again, while Cameron considered this revelation. He was sure it wasn't an unusual wish for a little girl, and he couldn't help but wonder how Gabriella had responded to her daughter's statement.

"You could have made that wish come true for her," he felt compelled to point out. "All you had to do was acknowledge the truth about her paternity."

"I thought about it," Gabriella admitted. "Not because it was Sierra's wish, but because I wanted her to know her father, and for her to know you."

"Then why didn't you?" he demanded. "If you really wanted me to know, why didn't you ever make any effort to contact me? Why is it that the only reason I found out about my daughter is that I tracked you down and came face-to-face with her?"

She glanced away. "I couldn't get in touch with you."

He scowled. "Are you claiming you didn't know how to reach me?"

"No, I'm saying that I couldn't. Because I'd made a promise."

"What kind of promise?" he demanded. "To whom?"

"Gabriella—"

They both started at the interruption.

"—are you bringing the cake?" Katarina's question preceded her entry into the kitchen. "Oh." She glanced from Gabriella to Cameron and back again. "I didn't realize I was interrupting."

"You're not," Gabriella responded quickly. "I was just looking for the matches."

"In the cupboard over the fridge, where we've always kept them," her mother pointed out.

"Right." Gabriella moved away from him, rising onto her tiptoes to retrieve the long box.

Cameron hovered in the background, feeling uneasy under the older woman's scrutiny. He'd never had occasion to meet Gabriella's mother before. When he and Gabriella had first started seeing each other, they'd each had their own reasons for wanting to keep the relationship a secret. He wondered if Gabriella had ever told her mother that he was Sierra's father, and guessed not. Katarina looked like the kind of woman who would have tracked him down and kicked his ass to hell and back if she'd known. But he also guessed, based on the narrow-eyed stare that pinned him now, that she'd figured it out—or at least had some suspicions.

"You must be Gabriella's mother." He thought about offering his hand, but decided against it as she looked more inclined to swat it away than accept it. "I'm Cameron Leandres."

"I know who I am and who you are," she said. "I didn't come in to exchange pleasantries, only to check on the cake."

"*Madre!*" Gabriella chided, her cheeks coloring slightly.

"I will **not apologize** for speaking my mind," Katarina told her. "And while I appreciate that you are Sierra's mother and want what is best for her, I don't see how encouraging a relationship between your daughter and this man—a man who wasn't there for you, who did nothing to help when your baby almost died—could be best for her. It would be far better for her to never know the identity of her father than to know he is a man who could turn his back on the girl he got pregnant and the innocent child she bore."

He didn't respond to Katarina's outburst but turned to Gabriella for clarification. "What does she mean—your baby almost died?"

But she only shook her head, shooting an angry look at her mother. "I'm *not* going to do this now."

"Dammit, Gabriella. I deserve to know—"

"Today is a celebration," she interrupted, her voice deliberately calm as she tucked the matches under arm and picked up the cake. "And Sierra is waiting."

So he bided his time. He wasn't particularly happy about it, but he waited. He watched the birthday girl blow out her candles and eat her cake, saw her kiss her grandmother's cheek and wrap her arms—cast and all—around her mother. There was such easy affection between the three women, evidence of the solid bond between all of them.

Gabriella had given their daughter a good life—with help from her mother, of course—and Sierra was obviously happy. What right did he have to barge into their lives at this late date and upset the status quo?

Yes, he was Sierra's father, but that was an accident of biology rather than any particular planning on his part. As Katarina pointed out, he hadn't been there for Gabriella through her pregnancy or childbirth or any of the other stages of Sierra's life until now. And why was he here now?

He frowned over that question as he helped Gabriella tidy up the kitchen. She was right—he hadn't been ready to be a father sixteen years ago, and he wasn't entirely sure he was ready now. But he was thirty-six now—old enough and mature enough to own up to his responsibilities, to be a father to his daughter—even if she didn't seem to need him.

He looked through the window over the sink. Most of the guests had already gone, but a few of Sierra's closest friends had lingered, along with a guy who was—in his opinion—far too close to his daughter.

"Who's that with Sierra?" he asked Gabriella.

She squeezed out the dish cloth, wiped around the outside of the sink. "Paolo."

He didn't want to ask, but the question sprang from his lips anyway. "Boyfriend?"

She nodded. "They've been seeing each other for about six months now."

"Isn't she too young to have a boyfriend?"

"She's sixteen," she reminded him.

"Just turned sixteen," he shot back.

She only smiled. "Paolo's a good guy."

He frowned. "Are you really okay with this?"

"Let's just say that I've learned to pick my battles."

"You seem to have a really good relationship," he commented. "I can't imagine you having any battles."

"If you stick around long enough, you'll see plenty of them," she promised.

"But you don't think I will stick around, do you?"

She was silent as she carefully folded the dish cloth, then draped it over the faucet. "I don't have any expectations one way or the other."

"I guess I can't blame you for that," he said. "But I can promise you that I'm sticking around this time."

"Because you think it's the right thing to do?"

"Partly," he admitted.

"But what if it's not?" she challenged.

"What do you mean?"

Her gaze went to the window, and when she finally turned back to him, he saw the confusion and uncertainty clearly in the depths of dark eyes. "What if telling Sierra the truth about who you are isn't the right thing for her?"

"Would you be asking that question if I wasn't a prince?"

Her hesitation confirmed that his title was a concern to her. Most people wanted to exploit his royal status; Gabriella would prefer it didn't exist.

"The fact is, you are a prince," she said. "And when word gets out that you have an illegitimate child, there will be a media frenzy with Sierra at the center."

"She'll deal with it," he said confidently.

"But why should she have to?"

"Because whether you want to acknowledge it or not, she is a Leandres, a princess and a member of the royal family of Tesoro del Mar."

"I'm not the only one who might not want to acknowledge it," Gabriella warned him.

"What's the supposed to mean?"

She shook her head. "Nothing. Forget it."

"Obviously it was something," he said. "And I'm growing frustrated by the way you continually dodge my questions."

"I'm not dodging," she denied.

He lifted a brow. "Just picking your battles?"

She gave him a half-smile. "Something like that."

"If you're not dodging, then tell me what your mother meant about Sierra almost dying."

"It really wasn't as dramatic as that," Gabriella said.

"Sounds like a dodge to me."

"She was born with an atrial septal defect—more commonly called a hole in the heart," she finally admitted. "It wasn't anything that was immediately apparent. She came out crying and she had ten fingers and ten toes, but her skin had a slightly bluish tinge and she seemed to struggle a little with her breathing, something that became more apparent during nursing.

"When it was diagnosed, the doctors were optimistic that it would close on its own. But it didn't, and when she was six months old, she had open heart surgery."

"Why do I get the feeling you're glossing over a lot of details?"

"Because I am. Because I really don't want to go back to that time, even in my mind, and remember how terrified I was."

He couldn't blame her for that. And he could understand why her mother resented him. Katarina was right—he hadn't been there for Gabriella, he'd done nothing to help when her baby had almost died, and now he'd stormed back into the life she'd built for herself and her child and was threatening to turn it upside down.

"The worst thing," she said to him now, "was knowing that Sierra needed the surgery and not knowing if the doctors would do it."

"Because she was so young?"

She shook her head. "Because I couldn't pay for it. I had no medical coverage, no savings." She looked down at the hands that she'd linked her lap. "I had nothing but my baby, and I was so scared I was going to lose her."

He couldn't even begin to imagine. Even now, only knowing about his daughter for a few weeks, he would be devastated if anything happened to her. Gabriella had carried their child in her womb for nine months, she'd struggled through he-didn't-know-how-many hours of labor to bring her into the world, and then she'd been given a medical diagnosis that forced her to face the possibility that her baby might die.

"But they did the surgery," he said, trying to refocus her thoughts on the positive outcome rather than the obstacles she'd faced.

She nodded. "I would have done anything, given anything, to save my baby."

Something in her voice alerted him to the fact that there was more to the story, some other detail that she wasn't telling him, something that he wasn't sure he wanted to know. "But you didn't come to me," he noted.

"No," she admitted. "I couldn't."

He didn't understand. She had to know that money wasn't an issue for him. Not only could he have taken care of the bill for Sierra's surgery, he could have bought a hospital—and would have—if it was necessary.

Maybe, after the way things had ended, she'd decided that she couldn't count on him for anything. But by her own admission, she'd been alone and scared and desperate. It seemed to him that desperation would have trumped everything else, and yet she still hadn't come to him.

"Why not?" he demanded.

She met his gaze evenly. "Because I'd made a deal with your mother."

Gabriella's tone was matter-of-fact. She refused to feel any guilt for what she had done and the only regret she had was that it had been necessary. But she'd meant what she said—she would have done anything to save her baby. And when the princess royal had visited her in the hospital and offered the chance to do just that, there had been absolutely no doubt in her mind.

She'd wondered about the other woman's motives in offering to help. Elena Leandres had made it clear to Gabriella the first day she visited the hospital that she didn't for one minute believe that Cameron was Sierra's father, although she'd kept close tabs on her son and knew about the weekend he'd spent with Gabriella. And she'd warned Gabriella of the havoc she would wreak if she ever dared suggest otherwise.

Gabriella knew it wasn't an empty threat. She knew it didn't matter that she hadn't ever been with anyone but Cameron. The truth had no force compared to a royal decree and if the princess royal claimed that she'd slept with a dozen men, any of whom could be the father of her child, she'd no doubt find a parade of men who would support her claim.

Gabriella resented the implication, but she didn't argue.

What was the point, anyway? Why should she insist on putting Cameron's name on her baby's birth certificate when he'd made it clear that he had no interest in her or the baby she carried? So she'd claimed the father was "unknown" and the princess royal had ensured that Gabriella had the money she needed to pay for Sierra's surgery.

It was, she'd thought at the time, more than a fair trade. And if she'd had occasional twinges of doubt over the years, she'd only needed to look at her happy and healthy daughter to push those twinges aside.

With Gabriella's confession, all of the pieces fell into place in Cameron's mind, like a jigsaw puzzle finally taking shape. Since coming face-to-face with his daughter that first day, he'd struggled to understand how Gabriella could keep their child a secret from him for so many years, why she would lie to him about Sierra's paternity. But now he knew. And long after he'd left the party and begun to drive the familiar winding streets that led to his mother's home, frustration and fury continued to burn inside of him.

Elena had already settled into bed for the night, the butler advised him, and Cameron knew she would not be happy to be disturbed. He didn't care. Nor did he wait in the parlor for her, as the butler suggested. He'd waited too damn long already.

Elena was just shoving her arms into the sleeves of a robe when he pushed open the door of her suite. She glanced over, irritation evident in the furrow of her brow. "Honestly, Cameron, do you have any idea what hour it is?"

"Just after midnight on the day of my daughter's sixteenth birthday," he noted.

Her hands paused in the act of tying a knot at the front of her robe. "So you know."

He stared at her, incredulous. "That's all you can say?"

"If it were up to me, we wouldn't be having this conversation at all," she reminded him.

"How could you not tell me? How could you have known that Gabriella had given birth to my child—*your grandchild*—and not tell me?"

Elena sniffed disdainfully. "I only knew that you'd shown poor judgment in dating a commoner—a waitress, no less—who later had a baby. I had no way of knowing that the child was yours."

"And yet you went to visit Gabriella in the hospital, to see the baby."

"I was curious."

"Curious enough to have the baby's DNA typed?"

"I don't need to explain my actions to you."

He shook his head. He'd known his mother was manipulative and self-centered and yet, throughout the drive to her home, he'd dared to let himself hope that there was some reasonable explanation for what she'd done.

"You knew she was mine."

"All I knew was that you were careless and immature and irresponsible—no greater crimes than most young men are guilty of—and I didn't want you to be stuck paying for those crimes for the rest of your life."

"But it was okay for Gabriella to pay?"

"She wanted the child."

"How could you know I didn't?"

She laughed at that, though the sound was abrupt and without humor. "You were little more than a child yourself, neither ready nor willing to be responsible for anyone else."

"It wasn't your decision to make."

"You'd already made your decision, by finally ending your relationship with the little slut."

He felt his hands curl into fists. He'd never wanted to hit another human being and the fact that he had to fight against the urge now—and that the human being in question was his mother—made his stomach churn. Deliberately, he blew out a long breath and unfurled his fingers. "She wasn't a slut, she is the mother of my child, and you will speak of her with respect."

"I am your mother and you will speak to *me* with respect," Elena said sharply.

"I can't speak to you at all right now," Cameron told her. "Just thinking about what you did, your lies and manipulations, makes me ill."

"I did what was best for you and this family."

"My daughter is part of this family," he shot back.

Elena's eyes narrowed. "You've worked hard to get where you are now," she reminded him. "What do you think will happen to your image in the press and the future of your career if you try to claim that bastard child as your daughter?"

"Do you think I care?"

"If you don't, you're a bigger fool than I thought. And maybe that's partly my fault," she continued. "I let you be the spoiled prince for too long, trusting that you would find your purpose and direction when you were ready. And I thought you had found it when you joined Rowan's cabinet. But this renewed fascination with Gabriella and your sudden determination to be some kind of father to her daughter prove you're as unfocused as ever."

"Actually, I think I may have finally found my focus," he told her.

"Walk away from her," Elena said. "If you don't, you're going to lose everything."

Cameron walked away from his mother instead. Because he'd finally realized that Gabriella and Sierra were everything that mattered, and he wasn't going to give up on them and the future he hoped they could build together. Not again.

After Cameron had gone, Elena sat at the antique desk in her upstairs office waiting for the supervisor of her security detail. As she was considering the most appropriate course of action, her gaze fell on the silver tri-fold frame—a gift from her late husband that contained photos of each of their three children.

She'd been blessed with two sons, and she'd had dreams and ambitions for each of them. Unfortunately, her disappointment had been as great as her plans when first Michael and then Cameron had chosen to pursue his own path. Though she'd been frustrated, she couldn't pretend not to understand where the defiance came from. She herself had defied her father's wishes to make a good match for her when she'd run away to marry a farmer.

It had seemed so romantic at the time. And she truly had loved Gaetan, at least in the beginning. When he'd died, just a few months after his forty-seventh birthday, she'd grieved—and she'd felt released. The idealistic life she'd envisioned had been painted over by the reality of trying to build a life with a man who wanted different things than she did—and who made no secret of the fact that he disapproved of her plans for their sons.

But he'd been gone a lot of years before she'd approached Michael about making a play for the throne. Her eldest son had refused to even consider her proposition. She'd tried to make him see that he'd been meant for greater things than his little advertising company, but he'd been adamant that his career and his wife were all he wanted.

He didn't even plan to have children, a decision which Elena viewed not just as a disappointment but a betrayal. As the oldest son, he had a duty to provide an heir. He needed a son of his own to extend the royal line and carry the family name. But while Michael remained steadfast, Samantha was eventually persuaded. Unfortunately, when she finally did give birth it was to a girl, and then she'd died only a few hours later, leaving Michael alone with the burden of an infant daughter.

He'd taken his wife's sudden and unexpected death hard, and Elena allowed herself a moment to wonder if Michael had yet adjusted to the loss before she focused her thoughts on her second-born son. Cameron had always been more malleable, more eager to please. In his youth, he'd been occasionally irresponsible and frequently reckless, but for the most part, he'd fallen in line with her expectations. Aside from that brief rebellious period in college when he'd been sneaking around with Gabriella, of course, but she'd nipped that in the bud. She'd helped him see the error of his ways and convinced him that he was destined for bigger things.

She didn't regret keeping the existence of his child a secret sixteen years ago. She only regretted that he'd found out now. But far worse than his knowledge was his intention to publicly claim the child as his own—as if he couldn't see that such an announcement would be an unmitigated disaster. He'd skirted the edge of scandal too many times already, and it was quite possible that the revelation of his youthful indiscretion would be the final nail in the coffin of his political career.

It wasn't that Elena had a problem with Cameron being a father, although she'd naturally been disappointed by the child's gender. If she didn't know better, she might have thought that both of her sons had fathered daughters on purpose just to spite her. But at least Michael had been married to the mother of his child, and while Elena and Samantha had never been close, her son's wife had come from a good family, she'd been well-educated and she'd been both understanding and respectful of Michael's background.

Gabriella Vasquez was a completely different story. She'd been nothing more than a starry-eyed waitress who saw the young prince as her ticket to the easy life. The quickness with which she'd snatched at Elena's offer of money in exchange for her silence about the baby was proof enough of that fact.

And now, sixteen years later, she thought she could renege on that agreement without consequence?

No way in hell.

Chapter Nine

Gabriella was usually up with the sun, but the day after Sierra's birthday party, she slept late. So late, in fact, that she only awakened when there was a knock on her bedroom door. She lifted a groggy head from her pillow when her mother poked her head in the room.

"What time is it?" Gabriella asked, squinting to focus on her clock.

"Almost time for me to be leaving for mass," Katarina said, stepping into the room. "But I didn't want to go without checking on you first."

Gabriella pushed herself up in bed. "I'm okay. I guess I was just more tired out from yesterday than I realized."

"It was a busy day," her mother agreed. "And an emotional one."

She just nodded.

"I overstepped," Katarina said. "With your prince."

"He's not mine," Gabriella told her. "And I understand why you feel the way that you do."

"I was so angry with you, when you refused to tell me the name of your baby's father."

"I couldn't. I didn't dare. It was all too easy to imagine you storming the gates of his family's estate, demanding that he marry me and give his name to my baby."

"He should have married you," Katarina insisted.

"We were both too young to marry."

"But old enough to make a baby."

Gabriella sighed. "And don't you think I'm a little too old for this lecture now, *madre?*"

Katarina shrugged. "Perhaps. It's just that I look at Sierra sometimes and she reminds me so much of you that it's scary. She's so beautiful and willful and I worry that she will follow her heart as you did, and have it broken."

"A broken heart heals," she said.

"And yet, you have never loved anyone else," her mother noted.

Gabriella thought, fleetingly, of Rafe, and wanted to protest, but the words stuck in her throat. Her mother was right. As much as she'd wanted to love Rafe, to share her life and build a future with him, she'd never been able to give him her heart. Because she'd already—foolishly—given it away too many years before. "I have you and Sierra. I don't need anyone else."

"If I had known—" Katarina shook her head. "I should have known. I should have seen that you were in love and always making excuses to get out of the house."

"I was pretty industrious," Gabriella admitted.

Her mother nodded. "But he was older, more sophisticated and experienced."

"And I was blind and naive," Gabriella interjected. "I know, and I'd rather not go down that road again." She'd spent enough time, during the darkest hours of the night, remembering what she'd had, what she'd lost, and wondering how things might have turned out if both she and Cameron had handled the situation differently.

"He broke your heart." There was anger and accusation in Katarina's tone.

"He gave me my daughter," Gabriella said softly.

"You always did look on the bright side of things."

"And she is the brightest part of my life."

Katarina smiled and touched a hand to her daughter's cheek. "I know how you feel."

When her hand dropped away, Gabriella reached for it, held on. "I'm scared," she admitted.

"Of telling Sierra?" Katarina guessed.

"Of losing Sierra," she admitted softly. "He can offer her so much more than I can."

"Things, perhaps." Katarina waved a hand dismissively. "But he cannot love her more than you do, and nothing he can offer her now will undermine the solid foundation you have given her over the past sixteen years."

"I hope you're right."

"You believe, then, that he is planning to acknowledge that he is her father?"

"I think he would have done so already, if I hadn't convinced him to wait—to give Sierra some time."

"He doesn't strike me as the patient type," Katarina mused.

"Not at all," Gabriella agreed.

"Which makes me wonder if maybe I was wrong."

"About what?"

"About what he wants from you." Her mother's tone was quiet now, reflective, and made Gabriella squirm uneasily.

"He wants a relationship with his daughter," she pointed out.

"Maybe that's true," Katarina agreed, "but it might not be the whole truth."

"Care to explain that? Because it's too early for me to wrap my head around one of your riddles."

"It's not early at all," her mother denied. "In fact, if I don't hurry now, I will be late for church."

Then she dropped a kiss on her daughter's cheek and was gone.

After she'd taken a quick shower to clear the last of the cobwebs from her brain and tugged on some clothes, Gabriella made her way down to the kitchen, following the scent of the coffee her mother had already brewed. She knew that some of her friends and colleagues had wondered about her living arrangement—a thirty-four-year-old mother of a teenage daughter living with her own mother—but Katarina had truly been her rock, not just since that fateful day when the results of an over-the-counter pregnancy test had changed her world, but for as long as she could remember.

She'd been so scared to tell her mother that she was pregnant. Not because she worried that her mother would turn her out of her home, but because she knew she would be disappointed. She'd raised Gabriella with traditional values and morals, and learning that her unwed teenage daughter was pregnant was a slap in the face to everything she believed in. Still, she'd never wavered in her support of her daughter, and the only time they'd seriously argued was when Gabriella refused to reveal the name of her baby's father.

In fact, it was only a few weeks earlier, after Cameron's first visit to her home, that Gabriella had been shaken enough to confess the truth. Based on her mother's reaction to the news—and her uncensored comments to Cameron the night before—Gabriella had been wise to keep that information to herself for so long.

But now, the secret that she'd so closely guarded for so many years was about to be revealed. And she couldn't help but wonder how the princess royal would respond to that.

Gabriella had kept her end of the bargain—she'd never told

Cameron about his child. In fact, she'd gone one step further and denied that he was the father when he'd asked. She hadn't counted on Cameron making any further inquiries on his own, and she didn't think Elena would have anticipated such interest, either.

The doorbell rang as she was refilling her mug with coffee and she carried it with her when she went to answer the summons. Cameron was on the step, but unlike his first visit to her home two weeks earlier, this time she didn't hesitate to step back and let him inside.

"Coffee?" she asked.

"Please," he said, sounding desperately grateful.

She returned to the kitchen, pulled a second mug from the cupboard. "Cream? Sugar?"

"Just black."

She glanced over her shoulder as he dropped into a chair at the table. "You look like you had a rough night."

"I haven't slept," he admitted.

She pushed the mug across the table to him. "At all?"

He shook his head. "I haven't even been home. After I left here last night, I went to see my mother. And then I just drove."

"That's a lot of driving," she said lightly.

"I had a lot of thinking to do."

"Do you want something to eat? I could scramble some eggs."

He glanced up, the ghost of a smile hovering at the edges of his lips. "I must really look like hell if you're offering to cook for me."

"I don't cook," she reminded him. "Scrambling eggs doesn't count as cooking."

"In that case, I would love some."

Gabriella took a handful of eggs out of the fridge, cracked them into a bowl. She added some milk, a dash of salt and pepper, then whipped them until they were frothy.

"For someone who doesn't cook, you know your way around a kitchen."

"I can handle the basics," she assured him, setting a frying pan on top of the stove.

"Do you have a recipe that might make a serving of crow more palatable?"

She slid a couple of slices of bread into the toaster, then turned to him. "A recipe for what?"

"Crow," he said again.

"Are you planning to eat crow?" she asked him.

"At the very least."

Gabriella took the coffee pot to the table, refilled his mug. "Eat your breakfast first," she instructed. "Before it gets cold."

He picked up his fork and dug into the eggs. The meal was simple but delicious, and in minutes, he'd completely cleaned his plate.

"I owe you an apology."

"I appreciate the sentiment," she said. "But I'd rather focus on where we go from here than rehash the past."

"That's generous of you."

"Not really," she denied. "We've both made mistakes."

He nodded. "So where do we go from here?"

She folded her hands around her mug. "I know you're anxious for Sierra to know who you are."

"I am," he agreed. "But it might be better if we spent some time together first, getting to know one another without the father-daughter labels hanging over our heads."

"I think that's a good idea."

"Does she like boats?"

"She's never been on one," Gabriella admitted. "But she's usually game to try new things."

"Then why don't we plan an outing for Wednesday afternoon?"

"Wednesday?"

"School's out for summer break now, isn't it?"

Gabriella nodded. "Sierra wrote her last exam Friday morning."

"Good," he said. "My morning is booked solid with meetings, but I should be able to get away from the office by noon and there won't be nearly as much traffic on the water then as on the weekend."

Maybe it should have irritated her that he didn't ask about her work schedule, but the fact was that as long as she got her columns in to her editor on time, her hours were completely flexible. And the idea of spending an afternoon out on the water instead of in front of her computer was too tempting to resist. "Do you want me to pack a lunch?"

"No. I'll have my chef put something together for us."

"Well, then, I'm sure we'll eat better than tuna sandwiches."

He frowned at the obvious pique in her tone. "It bothers you that I have a chef?"

"No," she denied. "I guess it just reminded me that you aren't like the rest of us common folk." And she was glad for the reminder, because allowing herself to think otherwise could be very dangerous.

"I could fire him, if that would make you feel better," he teased.

"Yeah, because putting some guy out of a job would make me happy," she said dryly.

"I don't understand why my title and status are such an issue for you."

"Of course you don't, because you're the one with the blue blood."

"It's not quite as blue as Elena would like everyone to believe," he told her.

"Your father wasn't of noble birth?" she guessed, aware that his mother had a direct connection to the throne.

"My father was a farmer," he told her. "It was quite the scandal when they got married."

"She must have really loved him," Gabriella mused. But try as she might, she couldn't imagine the woman who had heartlessly bargained with Sierra's life caring that much about anyone.

"Or she really wanted to piss off her father," Cameron suggested.

That scenario was much easier for Gabriella to envision. It also made her wonder, "Is that why you were with me?"

"I was with you because you were beautiful and sexy and smart," he said patiently. "And because the moment I laid eyes on you, I didn't want to be with anyone else."

The words sounded good, and Gabriella wanted to believe them. She wanted to believe in *him*. But she couldn't help remembering how careful he'd been to ensure they weren't seen in public together.

At the time, she'd thought he was protecting her from the media spotlight. Later, she'd accepted that he'd been protecting himself. After all, it would have damaged his image to be seen in the company of a waitress.

Sixteen years later, not much had changed. Although "the partying prince" didn't grace the covers of the tabloids as frequently as he had ten years earlier, he was still accustomed to being photographed in the company of the world's most wealthy and beautiful women. Gabriella didn't fit into either category. She was a single mother who had obtained her journalism degree while her daughter was in diapers and the simple fact that her child was also the prince's child couldn't magically bridge the distance that separated their two worlds.

"How many staff do you have on your yacht?" she asked him now.

"Three."

"Do you trust them?"

"Implicitly," he assured her without hesitation.

"Then I guess we'll see you around noon on Wednesday."

On Tuesday, the long-standing trade agreement between Tesoro del Mar and Ardena was officially renewed. Afterward, Cameron tracked down the prince regent in his office.

"I'm going to play hooky tomorrow afternoon," Cameron said.

"It's not really hooky if you tell me," Rowan informed him.

"Okay then, I'm not really playing hooky tomorrow afternoon."

Rowan pushed aside the document he'd been reviewing. "Obviously there's a reason you thought I should be aware of your plans."

"I just wanted to give you a heads-up, in case some enterprising photographer catches a picture of me and/or my guests."

Rowan waited, patiently, for him to continue.

"I'm going to spend the afternoon on my yacht with Gabriella Vasquez and her daughter—my daughter—Sierra."

The prince regent's brows shot up. "Your daughter?"

He nodded.

Rowan frowned. "Your personal life isn't any of my business—except when it reflects on this office. And when I appointed you to the cabinet, you promised me that you were finished living the life of a carefree playboy."

"And I meant it," Cameron assured him.

"Then can you tell me how in hell this happened?"

Cameron couldn't blame his cousin for being pissed. Because what Rowan hadn't said, but Cameron knew was that when he'd named his cousin to the cabinet, it was against the recommendation of several key advisors—and probably both of his brothers, too.

"A youthful indiscretion?" he suggested.

The furrow in Rowan's brow deepened. "Dammit, Cameron, you're thirty-six years old—"

"And she's sixteen."

His cousin's face drained of all color. "The mother?"

"*Dios,* no! My daughter."

"Oh." Rowan exhaled. "Thank God."

"I can't believe you'd even think—" Cameron shook his head. "That's just sick."

"I'm sorry." The apology was automatic but sincere. "I guess the headlines about the king's daughter are still on my mind."

"I only recently learned about Sierra's existence," Cameron explained. "And Gabriella and I have agreed to keep the truth of her paternity under wraps until we've had a chance to tell her."

"How many people do know?"

"Other than myself and Gabriella, just her mother, my mother, Marissa and now you."

"How did your mother respond to the news?"

"Let's just say that it wasn't news to her." Cameron's gut still burned with fury whenever he thought about his mother's lies.

Rowan, being well-acquainted with Elena's manipulations and machinations, only nodded. "Then I'd suggest you don't wait too long to tell your daughter," he warned. "Secrets have a habit of blowing up when we least expect it."

It was a truth that Cameron understood only too well.

"This is so lame," Sierra grumbled. She'd been on the phone with Beth, making plans to go down to the waterfront. They were going to spend the afternoon doing some shopping and hanging out, and then she was going to meet Paolo when he finished work.

It was, in her opinion, the perfect way to spend a summer

afternoon. Except that her mother had kiboshed those plans because she wanted Sierra to spend the day with her. Which wouldn't have been such a hardship, really. Gabriella was pretty cool, as far as mothers went. She didn't harp on Sierra all the time about her clothes or her make-up, the way Rachel's mother did. And she was usually flexible about her curfew, as long as she knew where Sierra was and who she was with.

But when Sierra tried to wriggle out of spending the afternoon with her, this time she was completely *in*flexible. And it wasn't even because she wanted some private mother-daughter time, it was because she wanted Sierra to get to know Prince Cameron. And maybe Sierra had thought it was sweet when she'd first met him and realized the man standing in her living room was royalty, but now, it was kind of weird.

She'd Googled him, out of curiosity, and she'd been stunned by the amount of information that was on the internet about him. The basic facts were well-known. He was the second son and middle child of the princess royal, Elena Marissa Santiago Leandres, and her deceased husband, Gaetan Rainier Leandres, which meant that Prince Cameron was fourteenth in line to the throne—not likely to ever rule the country but not completely out of the running, either, which was sort of cool. He'd been educated at St. Mary's College in Port Augustine and at Cambridge University and had spent several years traveling abroad before returning home to accept a position in the royal cabinet. His Royal Highness Prince Rowan Santiago, the current prince regent, had made the original appointment and recently named him the country's new Minister of Trade.

Aside from all of that, most of the other stuff she found was gossip—photos of women he'd dated, rumors of engagements, reports of break-ups. He'd dated *a lot* of women, but not any one woman for any length of time, and even if only half the stories she read were true (because she was savvy enough to know she couldn't believe *everything* she read on the internet), she felt that she had reason to worry about his interest in her mother.

Gabriella was every bit as beautiful as any of the other women he'd dated, but she lacked their worldliness and sophistication. Sierra couldn't help but wonder how her mother had caught his eye and what his intentions were toward her. And she decided that, as much as she resented having to change her own plans, it was probably a good idea for her to keep any eye on things.

Gabriella finished wrapping the plate of brownies. "I thought you would enjoy an afternoon on the water."

"With my mother and her new boyfriend?" she asked, not even trying to hide her sarcasm.

"It's not like that," Gabriella said. "Cameron and I are just friends."

Sierra wondered whether she was trying to convince her daughter or herself.

"I may only be sixteen," she reminded Gabriella, "but I'm not a child and I'm not an idiot. You dated Rafe for six months before you brought him home to meet me, now this prince is suddenly in your life and you're pushing me to get to know him.

"So is that the real reason you're dragging me along?" she pressed. "Am I your chaperone—so he doesn't pressure you to go too far?"

Gabriella pushed her hair back off her forehead and sent her daughter a baleful glance. "Honestly, Sierra, you have the most vivid imagination."

"I wasn't imagining the way he was looking at you."

"I'm not worried about Cameron behaving inappropriately," her mother insisted.

"Because you're as hot for him as he is for you?"

Gabriella's cheeks flushed. "Sierra."

It was her don't-mess-with-me tone and usually succeeded in getting her daughter to back down. But the color in her face confirmed that Sierra wasn't far off the mark. Not that she could blame her mother for being attracted—Cameron was incredibly good-looking, for an old guy, and he was a real-life prince, too. In any event, she knew there was more going on here than her mother was telling her, and she wasn't going to let up until she got to the truth.

Except that before she could say anything else, Cameron was at the door.

Chapter Ten

Twenty minutes later, they were at the harbor. Sierra didn't want to be impressed, but it was impossible not to be. She didn't know anything about boats and couldn't even have guessed at the size of the yacht—except to say that it was huge, and gorgeous. It shone brilliantly in the afternoon sun—as stunningly white as a pearl in the sapphire blue waters, and when she stepped onto the glossy wood deck, she felt as if she'd stepped into another world.

Cameron gave them a quick tour. She had expected that the inside would be dim, but it wasn't, as natural light shone through wide windows on every side. There was an enormous saloon with more glossy wood cabinets and tables with leather stools, cushy leather sofas and an impressive home theatre system, a small office, a master cabin with ensuite, plus two more guest cabins, each with its own private bath, and separate crew quarters.

While he'd been showing them around, the yacht had been making its way away from the island. When they finished the tour and returned to the main saloon, she was surprised by how much distance they'd put between themselves and the shore in such a short time.

"Are you hungry?" Cameron asked.

Sierra shrugged, trying to act casual.

"Starved," Gabriella admitted, shooting her daughter a look that Sierra chose to ignore.

"Good." He smiled at both of them, his even white teeth flashing white against his tanned skin. "Emilio has set up lunch on the deck, if that's acceptable. Or we can eat inside, if you'd prefer."

"Outside," Sierra answered automatically, before she remembered that she wasn't supposed to care.

"Gabriella?" he prompted.

There was something about the way he said the name that made it sound like a caress, and the color that infused her mother's cheeks confirmed that she'd heard it, as well.

"Outside sounds wonderful," Gabriella agreed.

He gestured for them to precede him, and again, Sierra had to give him points for presentation. The table had been set for three, with linens and fancy crystal and silverware that was probably the real deal and not the stainless steel stuff in their own drawer at home.

Cameron and her mother chatted easily over the meal, almost as if they really were old friends, and Sierra found herself wondering if maybe she'd been wrong about their relationship. But when he reached over and casually touched the back of her mother's hand and Gabriella's fork slipped from her fingers, she knew that she hadn't been wrong at all.

"Do you like to swim?" he asked, turning his attention to Sierra.

She nodded, because the fact that she did was one of the reasons she'd thought the afternoon on his yacht might not be a total bust.

"Then you should take a dip after lunch," he suggested, lifting his glass of wine. "The water out here is heavenly."

Yeah, he'd probably love for her to take a swim—while he put the moves on her mother.

"I can't swim," she said, holding up her arm in case he'd forgotten about the cast on it. Which he probably had, because he was too preoccupied with thoughts of getting her mother naked to worry about something as insignificant as her broken wrist.

"Sierra." Her mother's sharp response warned that she hadn't missed the disdainful tone of her daughter's voice. "Dr. Granger gave me some waterproof sleeves, if you want to go in the water."

The prince, to his credit, responded smoothly. "Or you could try the jet ski if you don't want to swim."

"Jet ski?" she echoed, her interest piqued despite herself.

"As long as it's okay with your mother," he hastened to add.

Now she did look at Gabriella, trying to convey a mixture of apology and pleading in her gaze. Her mother's hesitation was a warning to Sierra that she expected her best behavior from this point on. She gave a brief nod to telegraph her understanding.

"It's okay with me," Gabriella finally said. "As long as you have your cast covered and wear a life jacket."

Sierra opened her mouth to protest, then closed it again without uttering a word.

"Impressive," Cameron said to Gabriella later.

Lunch had been cleared away and they had taken their wine where they could watch Sierra who, now properly attired, was making waves out on the water.

"She's always loved the water," she told him.

"It shows," he said. "Although I wasn't talking about that."

Gabriella looked over at him. "Then what were you talking about?"

"The wordless communication between the two of you."

"It's not always as effective as I'd like," she said. "Which leads into my turn to apologize to you. She was being deliberately difficult and I don't know why."

"Don't you?"

"She's a teenager, which is probably enough of an explanation for a lot of her behavior, but it was more than that today."

"The 'more than that' being her feelings about the relationship between you and I?"

"That's exactly it," she admitted. "She's somehow got it into her head that we're more than friends and—"

"We *are* more than friends," he said.

The hand she'd raised to reach for her glass dropped away. "We have a history," she acknowledged.

"I think I understand now why she's worried."

"You do?"

He nodded. "Because our daughter is obviously more insightful than you are."

"Cameron."

"Gabriella."

She frowned at the amusement evident in his tone.

"After the kiss we shared in the park, do you really doubt that I'm attracted to you?"

"Considering your reputation, the fact that I'm female should be enough to assuage my doubts," she told him.

He shifted closer. "If you're trying to distract me by making me mad, it's not going to work."

"Didn't I make it clear, after that kiss, that you were wasting your time?"

"That's what you said," he agreed. "But I don't think it's what you meant."

She swallowed, glanced away. "I'm not playing hard to

get—I promise you. I just can't risk getting involved with you again."

"Because of Sierra?" he guessed.

"I want her to get to know you and have a relationship with you. But I don't want her to hope that we'll end up together like one big happy family."

"Because that's not what you want?"

Because it *was* what she wanted, more than anything. But she could hardly admit as much to Cameron. He'd already broken her heart once before—she wasn't going to give him the power to do so again.

"I'm trying to be realistic here, Cameron."

"Reality's overrated."

"Said the prince from his ivory tower," she retorted.

"Being royal has given me a lot of advantages," he acknowledged. "It has also presented a unique set of challenges."

"I'll bet none of those challenges included siphoning money from the grocery fund to pay the electrical bill so that the little food you had in the fridge didn't spoil."

"You're right," he admitted. "I can't begin to imagine how difficult it was for you, struggling to hold down a job and raise a child. And while I can tell you now that I would have helped, the words don't change anything."

"No," she agreed, then reached over to take his hand. "But thank you, anyway."

"I hate knowing that you didn't come to me because you didn't trust me not to turn you away. Because I had already turned you away."

"It was a long time ago," she reminded him.

He reached out, wrapped a strand of her hair around his finger, and tugged gently. The unexpected gesture threw her off-balance, and she had to step forward or risk stumbling.

"Gone but not forgotten?"

She had to tilt her head to meet his gaze, but pride wouldn't let her step away again. "What does that mean?"

"You keep saying that there's no point in dwelling on the past, that it's the future that matters. But you refuse to consider that we could have a future together, and I can't help but think that you're reticent because you haven't let go of the past."

"Maybe I'm reticent because I've never known you to talk about anything further into the future than dinner."

"Ouch." He dropped his hand from his hair, wrapped it around her waist. "So what if I did want to make plans for dinner?"

She could feel the strength in his arm, the heat of his touch, and had to swallow before she could speak. "We just finished lunch."

"We didn't have dessert."

"Sierra made brownies," she reminded him. Not that the brownies had been made specifically for this occasion, it was just that Sierra had been playing around in the kitchen and Gabriella had pilfered half of the pan to bring on this outing. Despite knowing that Cameron had a chef, she didn't like to show up empty-handed.

"Then we should wait for Sierra to have those. In the meantime…" His head lowered toward her.

Gabriella put her hand on his chest. "Don't play games with me, Cameron."

"Is that what you think I'm doing?"

"I don't know," she said. "My brain is spinning in circles right now so that I can't seem to figure any of this out. You invited us here today so that you could spend some time with Sierra—"

"And with you," he told her.

And when he looked at her like that, his eyes burning so intently with heat and hunger, she believed him. More, she felt herself responding.

"This is a mistake," she warned him.

But even before the words were completely out of her

mouth, the hand that she'd laid on his chest curled into the fabric of his shirt.

His mouth came down on hers, hard and hungry; her lips parted for him, eager and willing. She could taste the wine they'd both drunk, and the darker and more potent flavor of the passion that flared between them. Her hands slid up his chest, over his shoulders, linking behind his head. Her fingers toyed with the strands of hair that brushed his collar, so soft and silky in contrast to the lean, hard body pressed against hers.

She felt weak and hot and dizzy, and though she wished she could blame the hot Mediterranean sun, she knew her response had nothing to do with the weather and everything to do with the man. She'd always responded to him like this, completely and instinctively. And while she'd once thrilled to the discovery of such intense and all-consuming desire, she was embarrassed and ashamed to realize that she could still feel such depth of emotion for a man who had broken her heart—and a lot of other hearts, too.

He was used to having whatever he wanted, whenever he wanted, women included. She had been one of those women once, willingly and happily, but she wouldn't let herself be cast in that same role again. Not just because she wanted to protect her heart, but because she wanted to provide a better example for her daughter.

The daughter who, even now, could be on her way back to the boat.

She pulled away from him. "I can't do this."

Cameron took a minute to draw in a breath before he responded. "I'd say we were doing just fine."

"We both know how to go through the motions," she agreed. "But it's never been just that for me. I can't separate the wants of my body from the needs of my heart."

"And you assume that I can?"

"I'd say that history speaks for itself."

"Gone but not forgotten," he said again.

She shook her head. "I'm not referring to our history but your reputation."

"Deserved or not?" he challenged.

"Cameron, I work in the newspaper industry. I know as well as anyone that information is sometimes slanted, the truth is often stretched, and headlines are frequently exaggerated. But I also know it's a fact that you've dated more women in the past year than a lot of men date in their entire lifetimes."

Cameron had never been particularly concerned about his reputation, nor about the fact that it had been greatly exaggerated through the media. He enjoyed spending time in a woman's company, and he'd been fortunate that a lot of women seemed to enjoy his company in turn.

"But not one of those women—not any one that I've ever dated, in fact—has ever made me forget about you," he told Gabriella.

"Cameron, we haven't had any contact in more than sixteen years." She spoke patiently, as if she was talking to a dim-witted child. "You probably didn't even remember I existed until the photos of you with Princess Leticia were published."

She was wrong, but he didn't know how to convince her of the truth. He could hardly blame her for being skeptical. After the weekend they'd spent at Cielo del Norte, he'd realized that he was more than halfway in love with her—and he'd panicked. He was only twenty years old, still in college and with no real direction for his future—what did he know about love? How could he know for certain that she was "the one" when there were so many women out there? So many women who wanted to be with him?

He'd decided to take some time to figure things out. He'd promised to call her, but he didn't. As anxious as he was to hear her voice, he refused to give in, refused to admit—even to himself—how much he needed her. Because needing some-one was a weakness, and weaknesses could be exploited, and those of royal blood could not afford to be weak.

The day that she'd tracked him down on campus, he'd been so happy to see her, but he'd pretended that he didn't even remember her name. He'd been deliberately cruel, acting as if the time they'd spent together had meant nothing to him. And still, she'd had the courage to look him straight in the eye and confide her suspicion that she might be pregnant. That was when the real panic had set in.

Afterward, he'd thrown himself at other women, desperate to forget about Gabriella. Eventually, over time, the memories faded. But he'd never truly forgotten her. No one else's arms had ever felt so right around him, no one else's kisses had ever touched him so deep inside. No one else had ever loved him as freely and unconditionally as she had done, if only for a short while.

He'd been such a fool. He'd missed out on so much time with Gabriella—and the entire first sixteen years of Sierra's life—because he'd been a selfish and self-centered fool. That was time that he could never get back and, because he'd so completely and effectively isolated Gabriella so many years before, it was entirely possible that he'd blown any hope for the future, too.

"I guess it's going to take some time to convince you that I'm not the man the press has portrayed me to be."

"You don't need to convince me of anything," she said. "But if you say you want a relationship with Sierra, you better mean it. She needs a father who will be there for her, even—or maybe especially—when she's pretending that she doesn't need you at all."

"I'll be there for her," he promised.

And I'll be there for you, he silently vowed. *Even when you're pretending that you don't need me at all.*

The sound of the jet ski grew louder, signaling Sierra's

return. "Why don't you and I take that swim Sierra claimed she didn't want?" he suggested. "Then maybe she'll be enticed to join us."

"The water does look inviting," Gabriella admitted.

"Go put on your bathing suit," Cameron encouraged.

While she was changing, he did the same, and they were both ready by the time Sierra had returned. She declined the invitation to join them, opting instead to plug into her iPod and blast out her eardrums. Cameron decided that she needed some time, and turned his attention to the woman by his side.

"Maybe we should just head back," she suggested. "I know this day isn't turning out quite how you'd planned."

"I have no complaints," he assured her. "Unless you renege on your promise to go swimming with me."

With a shrug, she pulled off her cover-up. It dropped onto the deck—right beside Cameron's jaw.

Even at seventeen, Gabriella had the kind of beauty that stopped men in their tracks and the type of body that inspired them to fantasize about her. And he'd spent a lot of long, lonely nights doing just that before he'd finally known the pleasure of that sweet, lush body stretched out beneath him, wrapped around him, moving against him. She was somehow even more beautiful now, her body even more lush and breathtaking. And while the two-piece bathing suit she wore was modest by current standards, just one glance and his blood— already pumping hard and fast through his veins—quickly detoured south.

Oh man, he was in trouble here. Big trouble. And he suddenly found himself questioning the wisdom of getting half-naked with a woman who had always turned him on more than any other. Not that he would tell her as much, of course. Because even if he was foolish enough to make such a confession, she would never believe him. It was going to take time— time and a concerted effort—to break through Gabriella's resistance and convince her that the feelings he had for her were real.

In the meantime, he would have to take a lot of cold showers. But a cold shower not being immediately available, he decided a dip in the Mediterranean would have to suffice.

He dove deep, relishing the coolness of the water as his body sliced through it. Kicking hard, he pushed himself deeper. He swam downward until his lungs ached with the effort of holding his breath in, then he turned abruptly and pushed hard toward the surface. He broke through and drew in a deep, shuddering breath—and felt something smack into his shoulder.

Blinking water from his eyes, he saw Gabriella was in the water with him. Her hair was dripping wet, and her eyes were huge in her pale face.

"Goddamn you, Cameron."

The relief Gabriella had felt when he broke through the surface was overwhelming, but her heart was still pounding too hard and too fast. For almost a whole minute or maybe even longer—it certainly seemed like so much longer—he'd been gone. One minute he'd been standing beside her on the deck, the next he'd executed a clean dive into the water, and then he'd disappeared.

She should have called for the captain. That would have been the smart thing to do. But she hadn't been able to think—she'd just acted, and apparently that meant flinging herself over the edge and into the water after him.

She'd gone under three times, mindless of the salt that stung her eyes as she desperately scanned the crystal clear waters for any sign of where he'd gone. And then, finally, she'd seen him. Not injured or unconscious beneath the surface, but determinedly swimming toward it.

Cameron frowned at her. "What's got you all bent out of shape?"

She stared at him as she continued to tread water beside him. "You were underwater forever. I couldn't see where you'd gone, if you'd hit or head on something and—"

"And you jumped in to save me?" His lips curved, just a little, as if he was amused by her instinctive response.

She wanted to hit him again. "I don't know why I bothered."

"I think you do," he said. "I think maybe, just maybe, all of your claims to the contrary aside, you still care about me."

"I would try to save anyone I thought was drowning."

"Hey." He moved closer, lifting his hands out of the water to cradle her face in his palms. "I didn't mean to scare you."

"Well, you did." This time she did smack him again. The violent action splashed more water, hopefully masking the moisture that swam in her eyes. "You big idiot."

"I'm sorry." He dipped his head, brushed his lips lightly against hers.

She wanted to cling to him, to hold him and feel the solid warmth of his flesh beneath her hands. But she didn't, because to do so would only prove what he already suspected—that she still cared about him. And while she might be able to convince herself that it was perfectly normal and reasonable to care about the man who was the father of her child, she knew that her feelings for Cameron weren't that simple or straightforward.

"Stop that." She started to pull away, but he caught her, tangled his legs with hers. Their bodies bumped, once, twice, and the slick slide of wet skin against wet skin was incredibly and unbelievably arousing.

"I can't." His hands slid down her back to curl around her bottom and pull her closer. "I've tried, really I have, but I can't stop myself from wanting you."

The words, the tone, and the man were far too seductive—or maybe she was far too naive, because she wanted to believe he meant what he'd said. Because then it might be okay to admit that she wanted him, too.

"This is crazy," she said instead.

"You've always made me crazy." He nibbled his way along her jaw, down her throat, as they bobbed in the gentle waves.

"I thought we were going to swim."

"This is so much better than swimming."

"Right now, I'm having a hard time disagreeing with that," she admitted. "But this isn't the time or place."

Cameron suckled on her earlobe. "So tell me when and where."

His voice was warm with desire, silky with promise, and far too tempting. But somehow Gabriella resisted the impulse to let her head fall back, to let him lead where she was only too willing to follow. Because she'd been down that road before, and she'd found herself alone at the end.

"You make it sound so easy," she said.

"It could be," he told her.

She shook her head as she disentangled herself from him. When he was touching her, she couldn't think straight. When she was wanting him, she couldn't remember all the reasons that she shouldn't. "*I'm* not easy," she told him. "Not anymore."

"I never thought you were easy," he denied. "And I always believed you were worth the effort."

"I have to get back." She started swimming toward the ladder.

Cameron matched her, stroke for stroke. "You're running away."

"No. I have a column to finish and send in to my editor."

He was right behind her as she climbed out of the water.

"How about dinner?" he asked, as she started to towel off.

"I told you—I have work to do."

"Not tonight," he said. "Saturday."

She hesitated. "I think Sierra has plans with Paolo."

"I'm not asking Sierra, I'm asking you."

"I'd have to check my calendar."

"I'm trying to prove that I'm capable of thinking long-term," he told her. "Not just as far away as dinner, but dinner three days in the future."

"Should I be impressed?"

"You should say 'yes.'"

"Don't you need to check your calendar?" she challenged, knowing that his professional obligations—and his social life—were far more demanding than hers.

"No," he replied, without hesitation. "Because even if there's something else on my schedule, it couldn't possibly be as important as taking you to dinner."

He had the right answers to all of her questions, which only made her more cautious. He'd always been a player, and she couldn't take the chance that he was playing her—again.

"I think being here with you today is enough tempting of fate for one week."

"Would it really be so terrible to be seen in public with me?"

She'd always thought he was the one who didn't want to be seen with her. But now, she was wary. "It's not you, Cameron, it's the paparazzi that follows wherever you go. And I don't want my daughter reading headlines that label me as your latest conquest just because we were having dinner together."

"Our daughter."

She cast a glance toward Sierra, relieved to see that she was still listening to her iPod and apparently oblivious to their conversation. "Our daughter," she murmured in agreement.

"I promise you, no one will know where we're going and there will be no paparazzi hiding anywhere in the shadows waiting to snap pictures of us."

"How can you make that kind of promise?"

"Trust me," he said. "I've not only lived most of my life in the spotlight, I've learned how to court that attention when it serves my purpose—and how to circumvent it when necessary."

Still she hesitated.

"Seven o'clock," he suggested.

She sighed. "Okay. But I have to be home by midnight."

"Is that your curfew?" he teased.

"It's Sierra's, and I need to be home to know that she is."

"Then I will have you home by midnight," he promised.

Chapter Eleven

Dear Gabby,
The first time I fell in love, I was fifteen years old.
Maybe I was naive to believe that Carlos and I would
last forever, but he claimed to love me, too, and we spent
hours talking about the future. After high school graduation, we went to different colleges, but I continued to
believe that we would get back together again when we
both finished school. Except that when Carlos finally
came home, he was married to someone else.

I was devastated, but because I didn't want anyone to
know how heartbroken I was, I started dating someone
else. After a while, I convinced myself that I was in love
with him and, within a few months, we were married.
It took less time than that for me to realize that our
marriage had been a horrible mistake and that I'd never
stopped loving Carlos.

A couple of years ago, our paths crossed again. I
immediately realized that I still had strong feelings for

him. And since it turned out that he was divorced, too, it almost seemed natural to start dating again. We've been together now for almost a year and a half, and Carlos has been starting to drop hints about the two of us getting married.

I have never loved anyone else as much as I loved him, but no one else has ever hurt me as much as he did, either. I'm afraid to give him another chance, afraid that he'll break my heart all over again.

Should I play it safe—or risk it all for a chance to live happily-ever-after?
Signed,
Still Sorting Out the Pieces

Over the years that Gabriella had been writing her "Dear Gabby" column for the newspaper, she'd occasionally found that a reader's questions and concerns reflected current events in her own life. Those were always the most difficult letters to respond to because they required not just a dose of common sense but a fair bit of introspection and Gabriella wasn't always willing to look into herself. It was far easier, in her opinion, to respond to other people's problems than examine her own.

In this case, however, the issue was one at the forefront of her mind. Cameron had been more than hinting about wanting a second chance, and Gabriella was still reluctant to even consider the possibility.

Dear Sorting,
A man who can abuse your trust and break your heart once shouldn't be given a chance to do so again.

Gabriella sat back and studied the words on the screen. It was a valid point, she thought, but not quite the response that her readers expected. On a sigh, she held down the backspace key until the screen was blank again. Because as justified as she might have felt in writing those words, they were a personal response rather than a professional one.

Don't think about Cameron, she reminded herself. *Don't think about the fact that he claimed to love you and then dumped you. Don't think about the fact that he disappeared from your life for more than sixteen years and now expects to pick up right where things left off.*

She pushed him out of her mind—or at least tried to—and focused on her response again.

Dear Sorting,
There is nothing quite as intense as first love. And nothing quite as devastating as a first heartbreak.

It's not surprising that you would still be holding on to your hurt and using it as a shield to protect your heart this time around. But you and Carlos are different people now than you were in high school. You're not just older and more mature, you've lived separate lives and had distinct experiences, taken different paths that have merged to bring you together once again.

It's time to let go of the past and look to the future—and decide if you want him to be part of that future. It's not always easy to forgive and forget, and only you can decide if you're ready to take that next step.

The only thing I'll add to that is that second chances are rare. If you decide you want this one, grab hold of it with both hands.
Good luck,
Gabby

It was good advice—objectively, she knew that was true. But did she have the courage to listen to her own guidance? Did she want a second chance with Cameron? Or was she a fool to think he was even offering her one?

Had he really changed—or was he just playing her? He claimed that he wanted to be a father to his daughter, and Gabriella had no intention of standing in the way of that.

So what was his interest in her?

There was no shortage of women wanting to be with him, and no reason for Cameron to be with Gabriella unless that was truly what he wanted.

But what did *she* want?

She pondered that question as she rifled through the clothes in her wardrobe.

She wanted Sierra to have a relationship with Cameron, but she was also afraid to acknowledge that relationship. As soon as the truth came out, everything would change. Sierra wouldn't be her little girl anymore—she'd be the prince's daughter and a princess in her own right. Her life wouldn't be her own—she would be thrust into the spotlight, her every action and word scrutinized by the media. Gabriella wanted to protect her from that, for just a little while longer.

And yet, here she was—watching the clock and mentally calculating the time that she had left to get ready for her date with the prince.

Was she making a mistake?

She didn't want to think so, but the truth was, she'd never been able to think very clearly where Cameron Leandres was concerned. There was just something about the man that affected her on a basic level, stirring her blood and muddling her brain so that rational thought was all but impossible.

But she did know that playing it safe was no longer an option. She was playing with fire and she knew it. All she could do now was hope that no one got burned.

Cameron knew he was early, but he'd hoped that arriving ahead of schedule would give him a few minutes to talk to Sierra. The first time they'd met, she'd been obviously surprised and adorably flustered to realize who he was. Since then, however, her demeanor toward him had cooled noticeably. As he'd done nothing to justify this change in her attitude, he could only speculate that it was a reflection of her feelings about his relationship with Gabriella.

He thought he could understand her wariness. He knew that Gabriella had been dating Rafe for a long time, then suddenly Rafe was out of the picture and Cameron was in. And Sierra really had no idea who he was, aside from his title, and no reason to trust him or his motivations.

He heard footsteps approach in response to the ring of the bell, then Sierra was standing in front of him. The welcoming light in her eyes dimmed and her easy smile slipped when she recognized him. "Oh. I thought you were Paolo."

Gabriella had mentioned that Sierra probably had a date with the boyfriend tonight, and apparently she did. The teenager was dressed casually, in a simple knitted tank and a long flowing skirt that Cameron could easily picture Gabriella wearing. Obviously Sierra had inherited her mother's innate sense of style and—unfortunately, at least from a father's perspective—her ultra-feminine curves.

He wanted to suggest that she put on a sweater but knew she would look at him as if he was crazy. And maybe he was crazy to think that he had any business trying to parent a teenage girl that he'd only met a few weeks earlier. But it was more than a recently developed sense of responsibility that urged him to get to know his daughter, it was—from the moment he'd learned of her existence—an instinctive and irrefutable desire to claim her as his child. To be the type of father to her that he'd had been fortunate enough to have for the first dozen years of his life.

He forced himself to ignore what she was wearing and only said, "Can I come in anyway?"

Her cheeks flushed. "Yes, of course. You can have a seat in the living room. My mom should be down in a few minutes."

"Why don't you wait with me?" he suggested.

"Why would I?"

He wanted to call her on her rudeness, but he gritted his teeth to bite back the instinctive response and shrugged, deliberately casual. "It will give us a chance to get to know one another better."

Sierra paused in the arched entranceway of the living room and turned to face him. "Look, I know you're royalty and you're used to people bowing and curtsying. And I should probably be welcoming and gracious and oh-so-thrilled that you're dating my mother, but the truth is, I don't think you're good enough for her, even if you are a prince."

She spoke bluntly, unapologetically, and he was sure that Gabriella would be appalled if she heard the words coming out of her daughter's mouth. And while Cameron wasn't thrilled by her obvious lack of respect, he couldn't help but admire her strength of character and conviction. "You're probably right."

Her eyes narrowed suspiciously. "You're agreeing with me?"

"I've known your mom a long time," he told her, settling himself onto the sofa. "Although truthfully, in some ways, I hardly know her at all. But I do know that she's an incredible woman and I enjoy spending time with her."

"So that's all this is?" She folded her arms over her chest in a gesture that was so like her mother he had to fight back a smile. "Spending time with her?"

"We're taking things one step at a time," he said cautiously.

She inched a little farther into the room. "She was dating Rafe for almost two years. He asked her to marry him."

"Did you want her to marry him?" The idea sliced him to the quick. It was uncomfortable enough to think of Gabriella with the other man, but to imagine that her daughter—*his* daughter—had approved of that relationship and maybe even looked at the other man as a father figure, was unbearable.

But Sierra hesitated before answering, and he knew that she was considering her response. "I don't want her to be alone," she finally said.

"I don't imagine she thinks of herself as being alone."

"But I'm not going to be living here forever. I've only got two more years of high school and then I'll be going away to college. Hopefully."

Her frown warned that this was a subject of much debate between mother and daughter, and that no final decisions had been made. If it was a matter of finances, Cameron knew that he could alleviate their concerns, but that was hardly a discussion he intended to initiate now.

"And my grandmother's great," she continued. "But, come on, she shouldn't live with her mother forever, either."

He couldn't help but smile at that.

"And she doesn't have a lot of experience with men," Sierra confided. "I mean, I don't even remember her dating anyone, aside from Rafe. And you've dated a ton of women."

His brows rose. "Have you been reading the tabloids?"

"I did some internet research," she said, unapologetically. "And though I'm sure some of the stories are exaggerated, it's obvious that you've been around a lot more than she has."

"You're right," he acknowledged. "And there's probably nothing I can do or say to alleviate your concerns, but I can promise that my only intention tonight is to enjoy a quiet dinner with your mother."

"Okay." Then, almost reluctantly, she added, "She likes to dance. So you could maybe take her dancing, too, if you wanted."

"I'll keep that in mind," he promised.

"Okay," she said again.

The doorbell sounded, and her head turned automatically, her eyes lighting up.

"I need to get that," she said, just as her mother stepped into the room.

Cameron's attention shifted automatically, and his breath caught. Gabriella had put her hair up in some kind of twist and fastened simple gold hoops at her ears. Her make-up was mostly subtle—some shadow to highlight her eyes, a touch of blusher on her cheeks—aside from the mouth-watering red that slicked her lips. It matched the color of her dress, a sleeveless wrap-style of scarlet silk that dipped low between her breasts and clung to every delicious curve. And her feet were encased in shoes of that exact same shade that added almost three inches to her height and drew attention to her long, shapely legs.

Mi Dios, the woman knew how to tempt a man.

And he was more than tempted.

Thankfully, after a quick smile to acknowledge his presence, Gabriella had focused her attention on Sierra, giving him a moment to complete his perusal and recover his composure.

"Twelve o'clock," she reminded her daughter.

Sierra rolled her eyes. "As if I could ever forget."

Gabriella touched her lips gently to her cheek. "Have a good time."

"Yeah, uh, you, too." Sierra glanced past her mother to him, whether in acknowledgement or warning he couldn't be sure, but he knew that she was right to be worried. Because his promise to Sierra aside, one look at Gabriella, and suddenly he was wanting a lot more than dinner.

"You look…exquisite."

Gabriella felt her fingers tremble as the prince kissed her hand, and she hoped Cameron wouldn't notice. She was more nervous than she wanted to admit—like a seventeen-year-old girl on her first date.

"Thank you," she murmured.

He looked wonderful, too. But then again, he always did. The day they'd spent on his yacht, he'd been casually attired in shorts and a T-shirt. Tonight, he was wearing a suit—dark navy in color and conservative in cut. He moved easily, with a fluid grace and inherent dignity, whatever he was wearing and wherever he went.

It hadn't always been like that, she remembered. He'd once chafed at the restrictions that came with being a royal—except when he was outright ignoring them. He'd been the rebel prince, unconcerned with politics and protocol, determined to make his own mark in the world. And often, it had seemed to her as she'd followed his escapades through headlines over the years, desperately unhappy.

He had changed. She didn't doubt that any more. He was more comfortable in his own skin now, happier in his career and with his life. And she was happy for him—and hopeful that he could now be the kind of father her daughter deserved. But she was still unwilling to hope that he could be a part of her life.

He kept her hand in his as he led the way to the door. "Did you need to check in with your mother before we head out?"

She smiled, a little, in response to his gentle teasing. "Usually I would," she agreed. "But she's at her water aerobics class until nine."

"Water aerobics?"

"She loves to bake—and to eat what she bakes—so she does yoga or water aerobics almost every day, sometimes both, to balance it out."

"She sounds very…energetic," he decided.

"She only retired a couple of years ago," Gabriella told him, pausing to lock the door. "Until then, she'd worked two jobs. Having time on her hands was a huge adjustment for her."

"What kind of work did she used to do?"

Gabriella looked at him, surprised by the question. "I

thought you knew—she worked early mornings at the bakery and then cleaned houses the rest of the day."

He helped her into the limo, then settled himself beside her on the wide leather seat. "Why would I know that?"

"Because—" she broke off, shook her head. "It doesn't matter."

"My mother," he guessed flatly.

"I really don't want to talk about this tonight."

"Dammit, Gabriella. I need to know what she did."

"It won't change anything."

"No," he agreed. "But I'm tired of the lies and deceptions. I want the truth."

"When she first came to me, wanting to buy my silence with payment of Sierra's medical expenses, I refused. I believed, naively, that my mother and I would somehow find a way to pay the bills. The very next day, my mother lost her cleaning job at the Gianninis'."

"Elena and Roberta Giannini have been friends—or at least acquaintances—for years," he acknowledged.

She nodded. "And Roberta Giannini was good friends with Arianna Bertuzzi, so if my mother wanted to keep *that* job, I was told I'd better rethink my decision regarding Sierra."

He took both of her hands now. "*Dios,* Gabriella, I can't tell you how sorry I am."

"I hated her for a long time," she admitted. "And I was scared for even longer, afraid that the day might come when she wanted more than my silence."

"You were worried that she would try to take Sierra," he guessed.

"She'd already proven that she had the money and power and influence—all I had was my daughter, but she was everything to me."

He squeezed her hands gently as the limo rolled to a stop. "You were right. Let's try to put this aside for tonight and enjoy our dinner."

"Gladly," Gabriella said, and meant it.

The driver opened the door, and Cameron slid out first, offering his hand to her again.

She hadn't asked where they were going and, looking at the elegantly scripted letters on the huge plate glass window beneath the green-and-white-striped awning, realized now that had been a mistake.

But she never would have guessed—couldn't have guessed. Marconi's wasn't even in business anymore. After a falling-out with his son, Franco, who had moved to San Pedro to open his own restaurant six months earlier, Alonzo Marconi had closed down the business and put the building up for sale.

Cameron gestured for her to precede him up the walk, but Gabriella stood frozen in her tracks. "What are we doing here?"

"We're having dinner," he reminded her.

"But—" she faltered, as she caught a whiff of the tantalizing and familiar scent that drifted on the air.

"I promised to take you someplace where no one would guess we were going and where there would be no paparazzi hiding in the shadows."

"And you thought an abandoned restaurant would fit the bill."

"Not entirely abandoned," he assured her. "Alonzo Marconi himself is behind the stove tonight."

Still, she hesitated. It was obvious that Cameron had gone to quite a bit of trouble to set this up, but she wasn't entirely sure how she felt about this turn of events. She'd told him that the past was over and done, except that a lot of their shared past was now only a few steps away.

Already, just looking at the door, she could hear the familiar jangle of the bell that would sound when it was opened. And she knew that the sound of that bell would tear the lid off of the box of memories she'd worked hard to keep tightly closed.

Memories of the day she'd first met Cameron, the first time he'd kissed her. Memories of hanging out with him after the restaurant closed, talking for long hours or dancing to the music that blared out of the jukebox. Memories of hiding out in the bathroom, fighting against tears, after he'd dumped her, when she'd realized her period was late, and finally—when she'd been fired from her job after confiding to Mrs. Marconi that she was pregnant.

The memories were both plentiful and painful, and she knew that she could avoid them no longer.

Chapter Twelve

As Cameron followed Gabriella through the door, he began to wonder if he'd made a serious miscalculation. He'd thought she would be pleased with the arrangements he'd made, instead, she seemed apprehensive.

On the other hand, she'd seemed apprehensive since she'd agreed to have dinner with him, as if she'd been having second thoughts from the very beginning. But he was hopeful that he could get her to relax. They'd share a good meal together, an excellent bottle of wine, some pleasant conversation, and maybe, when the night was finally over, a good-night kiss.

He turned the key that had been left in the lock, so that no one could wander in off the street and disturb them.

She moved automatically toward the round table in the middle of the room, the only one that was set. The candle, stuffed into a squat wine bottle, had been lit, and the gentle flame illuminated the shine of flatware and the gleam of crystal.

"Something smells good," she said.

He agreed, although what he could smell was her scent, something light and citrusy, decidedly feminine and undeniably sexy.

"My sincere apologies, Your Highness." Alonzo Marconi rushed into the dining room, stopping in front of Cameron to execute a deep bow. "I did not realize you had arrived."

"It's not a problem," Cameron assured him. "And thank you again for your indulgence tonight."

"How could I refuse a personal request from a prince?"

A personal request—and the offer of a significant sum for the retired chef's time and trouble. But it was worth it to Cameron, to guarantee that he and Gabriella would have privacy tonight. He'd made her a promise, and he intended to prove to her that she could trust in his promises.

"You remember Gabriella?" he prompted.

"Of course." Alonzo took both of her hands before kissing her lavishly on each cheek in turn. "*Bella,* you are even more beautiful than I remembered."

"And you are just as charming as I remember," she told him.

"You are well? And your mother and your little girl?" he prompted, as he held out her chair for her.

"We are all very well, thanks. Although Sierra is not a little girl anymore. She had her sixteenth birthday last week."

"*Mi Dios*—where did the years go?"

As Cameron glanced around, he wondered the same thing. The restaurant hadn't changed at all in the six months that it had been closed. In fact, it looked to Cameron that not much had changed in the past sixteen years. Even the layout of the tables was the same, as familiar as the cane-back chairs set around them, the red-and-white-checked tablecloths draped over them and the candles in wine bottles that served as centerpieces for each one. The jukebox was still in the corner, silent now.

It had never been a high-end eating place but was undoubtedly an extremely popular one, having long ago established a reputation for serving quality food at reasonable prices. Primarily marketed as a family restaurant, it had also become a favorite of the college crowd, as it was located within walking distance of the dorms.

"I have the wine you requested," Alonzo told him, hustling over to the bar to retrieve it.

He hurried back, showed Cameron the label. He checked the date, nodded, and Alonzo quickly and efficiently uncorked the bottle. He poured a small amount in the prince's glass, allowing him to test and approve the burgundy before he filled Gabriella's glass. After topping up Cameron's, he set the bottle on the table.

"There is a set menu for this evening," Alonzo announced. "Crostini with basil pesto and tomatoes, followed by linguine with freshly made pomodoro sauce, then a main course of chicken piccata, finishing off with a simple green salad with an olive oil and red wine vinaigrette. And finally, for dessert, warm poached pears sprinkled with goat cheese."

"It sounds perfect," Cameron assured him.

Gradually, as they sipped their wine and nibbled their way through Alonzo's impressive menu, Gabriella began to relax. It helped, Cameron thought, that they talked mostly about Sierra. Although garnering more information about his daughter wasn't the primary purpose for the evening, he looked at the opportunity as a bonus. And Sierra was the one topic of conversation that seemed to break through Gabriella's reserve.

She happily recounted stories of Sierra's childhood, reported on every illness and injury, and detailed all of the important milestones of her first sixteen years until he finally formed a picture, not of the young woman she was now but of the little girl she'd been.

While he smiled at Gabriella's charming retelling of her antics, he was again painfully aware of how very much he'd missed. But he wasn't angry at Gabriella anymore. There was no reason to be. He knew now that he'd missed out on sixteen years of his daughter's life because he'd been too damned selfish and self-absorbed to worry about an ex-girlfriend's concern that she might be pregnant. Okay, so maybe he'd sweated over the possibility for a while. Maybe he'd waited to hear back from her, regarding the results of the pregnancy test. But when she'd failed to contact him again, he'd assumed that she'd been wrong—or that she'd taken care of it. And he'd been selfish and self-absorbed enough to be relieved by that thought.

Gabriella pushed away her salad bowl, the action drawing him away from the uncomfortable memories of his past and back to the much more enjoyable present.

"The whole meal was spectacular," she said. "But I can't possibly eat another bite."

"You have to have room for dessert."

She groaned. "I wish I did. Really. But—"

Her protest trailed off when Alonzo came out with the poached pears. Her eyes shifted to the square plate of neatly arranged pear halves drizzled with a Reisling reduction and sprinkled with goat cheese, and he could tell that she was tempted, at least a little.

"A few bites," he cajoled, after the chef had slipped away again. "So as not to hurt Alonzo's feelings."

"I'll have to start going to water aerobics with my mother," she muttered, but picked up her dessert fork.

He didn't think she needed to worry about indulging in a few desserts, but he refrained from saying so. He knew that kind of comment would catapult them out of neutral conversational territory into the decidedly personal zone and result in all of Gabriella's barriers locking firmly back into place.

She broke off a piece of pear, popped it into her mouth. Her lips closed around the tines of the fork, her eyelids lowered, and she hummed in blissful pleasure. "Mmm."

"That sounds like a positive endorsement," Cameron mused.

She nodded as she chewed, swallowed. "Oh. Wow. It's... fabulous. It's sweet and tart, and the cheese adds a little bit of creamy texture, and the flavors just explode on your tongue."

She sliced off another piece of fruit, held it out to Cameron. It was a spontaneous gesture, certainly not one that was intended to be deliberately seductive. But when his lips parted and she slid the fork between them, they were both suddenly aware of the intimacy of the moment.

She pulled the utensil away, her cheeks flushing. Cameron's eyes remained on hers as he chewed slowly, savoring the bite she'd shared with him. The air nearly crackled with the attraction between them, proving that the illusion of neutrality had been exactly that.

Alonzo bustled in again, offering coffee or tea.

Gabriella tore her gaze from his, and turned to smile at the chef. "Not for me, thanks."

"Nor me," Cameron agreed. "But I think we'll linger for a while, to finish up our dessert and the wine."

"Of course," Alonzo said. "If it's acceptable to you, I will come back tomorrow to finish cleaning up so that you will have some privacy."

Cameron nodded. "We'll lock up when we go. And thank you again."

"My pleasure, Your Highness." He bowed deeply to Cameron, then turned his attention—and a warm smile—to Gabriella. "And it's always a pleasure to see you, *bella.*"

"*Grazie, Signor Marconi.*" She touched his hand. "*Grazie per tutto.*"

He captured her fingers and raised her hand to his lips. "*Buona notte.*"

With a last bow, Alonzo slipped away, leaving them alone.

"Do you want to tell me what that was about?" Cameron asked.

"What are you talking about?"

"I'm talking about Alonzo flirting with you—right in front of me."

"He wasn't flirting with me," Gabriella denied.

"It sure looked like that from where I'm sitting—and that you were flirting back."

She shook her head. "I've known Signor Marconi for a long time," she reminded him. "In a lot of ways, he was like a father to me. He gave me more than a job—he gave me advice and guidance and support."

Her gaze shifted away from his, her fingers slid down the stem of her wineglass, traced a slow circle around the perimeter of the base.

"Obviously there's more to the story," he guessed.

"Let's just say that *Signora* Marconi was a little less supportive."

"His wife?"

She nodded. "She fired me. When she found out... Well, she said that this was supposed to be a family restaurant and that it wouldn't do to have an unwed, pregnant teenager waiting on tables.

"Alonzo was furious with her. He didn't approve of my condition any more than she did, but he understood that I needed some way to support myself and my child. So he gave me a new job—washing dishes." Gabriella shrugged. "The money wasn't as good as working in the dining room, but at least it was something."

"I'm sorry," Cameron said. "I brought you here tonight because I'd hoped it would help you remember the good times. I didn't realize how much history you had here."

"Most of it was good times," she said, then her lips curved a little at the edges. "Aside from the occasional night when I had to wait on tables filled with obnoxious college boys."

"You can't be talking about my friends."

"You guys used to take turns paying the bill," she recalled. "And I always knew when it was your friend Andre's turn, because I would find my tip—in nickels and dimes—in the bottom of the beer pitcher."

Cameron winced. "Okay. He was obnoxious. But another one of those guys used to hang around after closing sometimes, staying late to help you clean up—and just to be with you."

She frowned, as if she wasn't sure she remembered what he was talking about, but the teasing sparkle in her eye assured him that she did.

He pushed his chair away from the table and went over to the ancient jukebox against the wall. He dropped some coins into the slot, punched in the numbers from memory. He watched Gabriella as the first unmistakable notes of "Why Can't This Be Love?" filled the air. The half-smile on her lips faded, and every muscle in her body went still.

She'd been a die-hard Van Halen fan and when she'd locked the doors after the last customers had gone, she'd crank up the music and dance around while she wiped down the tables and stacked the chairs. The very first time he'd kissed her, it was this song that had been playing. Thinking about that now, he couldn't help but wonder how it was that he struggled to remember the names of half the women he'd slept with in the past dozen years, but he'd never forgotten a single detail of the time he'd spent with Gabriella.

"Dance with me."

She hesitated.

"Come on," he cajoled. "You don't want to disappoint Sierra."

"How does this have anything to do with Sierra?"

"She suggested that I take you out dancing. I know the ambiance here isn't the same as a club, there's no flashing lights or pulsing bass or—"

"No," she agreed. "This is better." Then she finally put her hand in his.

He drew her gently to her feet. She came willingly, if not quite eagerly. She was still wary, he understood that, so he would content himself with little steps. Right now, all that mattered was that she was in his arms.

It wasn't exactly a slow song, but they'd always danced to it like this, close together. They fell into that same familiar rhythm now, and with each whisper of contact, even the most subtle brush of flesh against flesh, the sparks between them flared hotter.

Less than two and a half minutes into the song, he gave up any pretense of following the music and settled his hands on those seductively swaying hips, pulling her hard against him. Gabriella's eyes widened, but her lips curved, and she lifted her arms to his shoulders.

There was no hesitation when he kissed her this time, and nothing tentative in her response.

Her lips were soft and yielding, deliciously and intoxicatingly familiar. Of course he remembered her taste—he'd kissed her on his yacht only a few days earlier. But he'd remembered her taste even then; he'd been haunted by her scent and her warmth and her passion for years.

There had been a lot of women in and out of his life over the years. Probably too many women. But none of them had ever lingered in his mind or taken hold of his heart the way Gabriella had done.

It was more than the rush of blood through his veins, it was the rush of joy he felt when she smiled at him. It was the way his pulse leapt when she so much as glanced in his direction, the way his heart pounded when she touched a hand to his sleeve. It was the unexpected and undeniable bone-deep contentment and rightness that he'd only ever felt when she was in his arms.

Seventeen years ago, he'd told her that he'd loved her. But

even when he'd said those words to her, even when his heart
had felt as if it would burst with happiness when she said them
back, he hadn't fully understood what they meant. He hadn't
fully appreciated the true depth of his feelings while he was
with her—and he certainly hadn't anticipated the intensity of
the emptiness he would feel when she was gone.

But she was here with him now, warm and willing, and he
had no intention of ever letting her go again.

He combed his fingers through her hair. Pins scattered as
the soft mass spilled down onto her shoulders. He'd always
loved her hair, the way it looked spread out over his pillow,
and the way she looked at him, sleepy-eyed and contented.
The image was sharp and vivid in his mind, and he wanted
her like that again. Now.

He tore his lips from hers to trail kisses down her throat.
He lingered at the racing pulse point at her jaw, and she sighed
with pleasure. He moved lower, tracing the deep V at the front
of her dress, dipping his tongue into the warm hollow between
her breasts. She shuddered but didn't pull away. He found the
tie at her waist, released it. There was another tie inside, but
he made quick work of that, too, and suddenly his hands were
inside the dress, on her bare, quivering flesh.

A quick glimpse of the red lace bikini panties and matching bra had him groaning aloud. She was so lush and perfect
and…his. He backed her up against the jukebox and curled
his hands around her buttocks, lifting her off of the ground.
She braced her back against the machine and wrapped her
legs around him, pressing herself more intimately against him,
and he groaned again as all the blood rushed from his head.

He unfastened the front clasp of her bra, letting her breasts
spill free. He filled his hands with them, brushed his thumbs
over the tightly-beaded nipples, and she gasped. He captured
her mouth again, his tongue sliding between her lips, tangling
with hers. Her hands were in his hair now, and the way she

was kissing him back and pressing against him left him in absolutely no doubt that she wanted the same thing he did.

There was no one else around. Alonzo had gone, the door was locked, and the blinds were drawn on all the windows. There was no danger of anyone seeing inside, no fear of anyone interrupting them, and he needed her desperately.

But he'd been careless with her before. So focused on his own wants that he'd barely considered hers. He'd been so hot for her that he'd taken her virginity in the backseat of his car. He had more finesse now, and a hell of a lot more self-control. Usually.

Somehow being with Gabriella undermined all of his best intentions. She made him forget that he wanted to do the right thing this time and simply made him want. But he wasn't going to take her standing up against an old jukebox. Or laid out on top of a checkered tablecloth. He reprimanded himself for the alternate suggestion that immediately sprang to mind. And so, with unbelievable reluctance, he lifted his head from her breast and refastened the clip at the front of her bra.

"Gabriella—"

She pulled away from him, her fingers trembling as she pulled at the ties of her dress. "Don't say it."

"Say what?"

"Anything." She tugged at the bodice, settling the material back into place, and shook her head. "I can't believe how pathetic I am."

He heard the tears in her voice, as baffling as her words. "What are you talking about?"

"Your mother was right—I am a slut. Maybe I've never slept around, but I've never been able to control my responses to you, either."

He stared at her, stunned not by what his mother had said but that she could possibly believe it. "*Mi Dios,* Gabriella. Allowing yourself to feel passion doesn't mean you're a..."

He trailed off, unable to even say the word. "It doesn't mean you're indiscriminate, it only means you're human."

"I almost let you seduce me in the middle of a restaurant." She had tears on her cheeks now and her eyes were filled with misery. "Is that why you brought me here?" she asked him now. "Did you figure I'd put out as easily now as I did seventeen years ago?"

"I didn't plan for this to happen," he told her.

She made a sound of disbelief as she finished tugging her skirt into place.

"But I'm not sorry. Because what just happened proves that the chemistry between us is as volatile now as it was seventeen years ago."

"It's not chemistry, it's hormones," she said derisively, but he sensed that she was more angry with herself than with him.

"Why are you so determined to fight this?" he asked gently.

"Because I don't do things like this." She swiped impatiently at another tear that slid down her cheek.

He tucked a lock of hair behind her ear. "Things like what?"

"Let myself be overcome by lust," she snapped at him.

She was trying to make the intimacy they'd just shared into less than it was, but he wasn't going to let her. "It's not about 'letting' when the attraction between two people is as strong as it is between us." He touched a hand to her face. "I've never felt this way with anyone else—before or after you."

"Are we done here?" she asked him.

He sighed. "And you're never going to give me another chance, are you?"

"Another chance for what?"

"To make a relationship between us work."

"We never had a relationship, we had sex."

"I loved you."

"Yeah, you made that clear when you dumped me after the weekend we spent together."

"I was young and stupid—"

"It doesn't matter," she said wearily. "Not the when or the why, because the truth is, the break-up was inevitable. Aside from the fact that we were both too young to have a clue about what we were doing, you're a blue-blood royal and I'm a working-class single mother."

"The mother of *my* child."

"Which might be my ticket to five minutes of fame but isn't going to lead to some kind of happily-ever-after."

"Not if you refuse to even consider the possibility."

She folded her arms over her chest, the action telling him more definitively than any words that she wouldn't be swayed, but she only said, "I need to be home before midnight."

"I'll have Lucien bring the car around."

Chapter Thirteen

Gabriella was on the back porch, watching the stars, when Sierra got home. While the midnight curfew was a matter of frequent debate between them, her daughter didn't seem to be holding a grudge tonight. Instead of ignoring her mother and going straight to her room, as she had a habit of doing when she was annoyed, she sat down on the step beside her.

"How was your date?" she asked.

"It was…" Gabriella wasn't quite sure how to respond. Both "wonderful" and "awful" were appropriate answers to the question, but either one would inevitably lead to more questions that she wasn't prepared to answer. So she only said, "Fine."

"Fine?" Sierra's brow furrowed. "Mom—if he can't do better than "fine," then you're wasting your time."

"Okay, it was better than fine," she allowed, not daring to let herself think about how much better specific parts of the evening had been. Specifically when her parts had been in close contact with his parts—

No, not going to think about those parts, she reminded herself sternly.

"Are you in love with him?"

Sierra's question startled her out of her reverie. She managed a laugh. "Love? Sierra, I've only been seeing him for a few weeks."

"But you've known him a long time, right?"

She nodded, because it was easier than explaining that she wasn't sure if she'd ever really known him at all.

"Did you date him?" Sierra prompted. "You know, when you knew him before?"

"Yes," Gabriella admitted, because while she'd never volunteered much information about her past, she'd never lied to Sierra, either. "For a little while."

"What went wrong?"

And how to answer that question without opening the floodgates? she wondered.

But maybe it was time to stop worrying about protecting Sierra and finally tell her the truth—to tell her that Prince Cameron Leandres of Tesoro del Mar was her father.

"We wanted different things from one another," she began, trailing off as she heard the sound of footsteps on the gravel driveway.

She glanced at her watch, noted that it was half past midnight. Sierra, obviously having heard the footsteps, too, was frowning. And they both jolted when a figure came around the side of the house.

Katarina stopped with her foot on the bottom step, her eyes wide. "What are you two doing out here at this time of night?" she demanded imperiously.

"I'd say the real question is what are *you* doing coming home at this time of night?" Gabriella countered. "Your car was in the driveway—I assumed you were home and in bed."

Katarina tilted her chin. "Well, you assumed wrong. As it turns out, I had a date tonight, too."

"With whom?" Gabriella demanded.

"With Dominic Donatella. Because I decided that I wasn't going to let him seduce the secrets of my buttercream icing out of me but I didn't mind if he seduced *me*."

"Go, Grandma," Sierra said approvingly.

Gabriella just shook her head. "Go to bed, Sierra."

Her daughter exhaled a long-suffering sigh, but she pushed herself to her feet, dropping a kiss first on her mother's cheek, then her grandmother's.

"Details over breakfast?" she whispered to Katarina.

"Not likely," her grandmother replied, but with an indulgent smile.

"I think I'm going to go to bed, too," Gabriella said, following her daughter toward the house.

"Have a cup of tea with me first," her mother urged. "I'm too wired to sleep right now."

Gabriella held up a hand. "Please, spare me the details."

Katarina picked up the kettle from the stove, filled it from the tap. "Obviously your date wasn't as…satisfying…as mine," she teased.

"No, I only *almost* had sex," Gabriella grumbled.

"That would explain your lousy mood," Katarina acknowledged.

"I should never have agreed to this dating charade. At first, it seemed like a legitimate way to explain why Cameron was hanging around while giving him some time to get to know Sierra. I didn't really think there would be any dating involved."

"And now you're worried that the lines between reality and fantasy are getting blurred," her mother guessed, all teasing forgotten.

Gabriella sighed, nodded.

"How do you feel about him?"

"I don't know. I don't know anything anymore."

"He's an attractive man," Katarina acknowledged. "A prince. And you were in love with him once before."

"A long time ago."

"Are you saying that you don't still have feelings for him?"

"I don't know. I mean, when I'm with him, he stirs up all kinds of feelings that I'd thought were dead and buried. I'm attracted to him," she admitted, although it made her blush to say the words aloud to her mother. Ridiculous, she knew, considering that her fifty-seven-year-old mother apparently didn't have any qualms about sharing the details of her sex life.

"But?" Katarina prompted.

Gabriella sighed. "But I don't know if I'm making those feelings into more than they are because I'm afraid of losing Sierra."

Her mother poured boiling water into the pot. "You're going to have to connect the dots for me."

"At first I was just going through the motions—letting Cameron hang around because I was sure that he would lose interest in playing daddy. But I've realized that he is serious about wanting to acknowledge Sierra as his daughter, and it's only a matter of time before he does so publicly. And when that happens, everything will change—for all of us, but mostly for Sierra. She will be a princess with royal duties and responsibilities, and I won't be able to help her with any of that. But if I'm with Cameron, well, it would ensure that I was able to stay close to her."

"Do you really think you could be that calculating?"

"Haven't I already proven that I will do anything for my daughter—even going so far as to keep her existence a secret from her own father for sixteen years?"

"Because the princess royal gave you no choice. Sierra

needed surgery, and she would only pay the hospital bills if you promised not to tell the prince about his child."

Gabriella nodded. "That's how I justified it to myself," she agreed. "But maybe it wasn't that simple. Maybe not telling Cameron about Sierra was a way of punishing him for dumping me."

"No one could blame you for being hurt or angry."

"But that doesn't justify using him for my own purposes now."

Katarina reached across the table to cover her daughter's hand with her own. "Are you really afraid that you're using him—or more afraid that you're not?"

"I can't fall for him again." Gabriella shook her head. "I won't."

"You say that with such conviction, as if you believe it."

"Because I do. Because it's true."

"Then you haven't learned anything at all in the past seventeen years," Katarina told her. "Because the mind does not and cannot control the heart."

Elena was growing weary of these late-night meetings, not so much the hour as the lack of results. In fact, she'd been more than a little tempted to cancel this one when she'd received Reynard's text message. "I think I've got something."

Elena had been as annoyed as she'd been intrigued. Her chief of security had been with her a long time, and he knew that she wanted results, not vague promises. Either he had something or he didn't—she wasn't interested in his thoughts.

Still, she was curious enough to keep the meeting, and she was waiting when Reynard appeared at the door precisely on schedule.

He knew her well enough not to waste any time on small talk, and as he made his way toward her desk, she could see that he had a small recording device in his hand. A touch of his thumb to one of the buttons and voices filled the silence.

Elena listened, definitely more intrigued than annoyed now. And when the playback finally ended, she nodded. "Yes, that should serve my purposes."

"Shall I arrange for a copy to be sent to his office?" Reynard asked.

She considered the idea for only a brief moment before discarding it. There wasn't a lot of time—with each day that passed, Gabriella was sinking her claws deeper and deeper into Cameron. Even though Elena had tried to warn her son about the kind of woman he was keeping company with, he'd refused to listen. His refusal had left Elena with no choice. She would do what was necessary to pull those claws free and if Cameron was left with scars, well, he would have no one to blame but himself.

"No," she finally responded to Reynard's question. "I'll deliver it to him personally."

Gabriella sat alone, thinking over her mother's words long after Katarina had gone up to bed.

She was right, of course. Not just about the fact that Gabriella couldn't stop herself from falling in love with Cameron again, but that the real root of her fear was the knowledge that she was already more than halfway there.

She should know better. She should have learned her lesson. But even if she didn't believe his claim that he'd loved her seventeen years ago, she did believe that he wasn't the same man now that he'd been then. And maybe, if he really did want a second chance and was willing to try to make a relationship between them work, Gabriella could make the effort, too.

She was scared, because there was so much more at stake now than just her heart. There was Sierra to think about—their daughter who didn't yet know that Cameron was her father.

There's no reward without risk, she reminded herself, and picked up the phone.

She faltered when she heard his voice on the other end. She hadn't expected him to answer, had anticipated leaving a message on his voice mail.

"I know it's late," she said.

"It's okay," he assured her. "I was still awake."

"Okay. Well, I, uh, wanted to apologize, for some of the things I said tonight."

"That's not necessary," he told her.

"It is," she insisted. "I was feeling emotional and vulnerable, and I lashed out at you."

"And I was pushing for too much too soon," he acknowledged.

"Maybe. A little." She blew out a breath. "Anyway, I thought maybe I could make it up to you, by inviting you to come over here for dinner. Tomorrow night."

"I thought you didn't cook."

"I didn't say I would cook, I said I would provide dinner. Actually, I thought I might be able to cajole my mother into cooking," she admitted. "But she's going away for the weekend, which means that I'll probably get takeout."

"Well, that's an intriguing offer," he said.

But he didn't immediately accept or decline, and Gabriella found herself babbling again. "It's short notice, I know. I should have realized that you probably already have plans. Or a date."

He laughed, although it sounded more strained than amused. "*Dios,* Gabriella, I don't have a date."

"Oh. Well."

"I was just…caught off guard by your invitation."

"It was an impulse," she admitted. "Probably a bad idea. Maybe we should just forget that I called."

"No way," he told her. "Just tell me what time tomorrow and I'll be there."

"Six? Seven? Whatever works for you," she said. "Although Sierra's going to a party with some friends tomorrow night, so if you want to see her, maybe you should come a little earlier."

"Earlier than six?"

"No, six would be fine."

"Then I'll see you at six," he promised.

"Okay."

She hung up the phone and wiped her damp palms on her skirt. She'd sounded like an idiot—worse, a babbling incoherent idiot. And yet, she had another date for tomorrow night.

She drew out a shaky breath and pressed a hand to her hammering heart. She was excited and terrified and determined. If this was her second chance, she was going to grab hold of it with both hands.

Cameron wasn't sure what had precipitated Gabriella's phone call, and he didn't care. He was just grateful that they seemed to have turned a corner, that she was finally willing to give him a second chance. He woke up the next morning with a smile that carried him through most of the day. The only snag was an early-afternoon visit from his mother.

There had been a time when he'd believed that Elena wanted only the best for him. He was no longer as trusting or naive, and he understood now that every action the princess royal performed and every word she spoke were carefully calculated to promote her own agenda. As she demonstrated with the recording she'd delivered to him that afternoon in an attempt to alter his intentions with respect to Gabriella and Sierra.

He'd been shocked to hear Gabriella's voice—and stunned by the words she spoke.

I will do anything for my daughter, even letting Cameron hang around. But I'm using him for my own purposes now, punishing him for dumping me. I won't fall for him again.

Elena claimed that Gabriella had spoken those words during a conversation with her mother, and listening to his own mother, he'd actually felt physically ill. Not because he believed what she was telling him, but because he was appalled by her actions. She insisted that she was only trying to protect him, but he saw the truth now: she was trying to control him, and she didn't give a damn about anyone else who might get hurt in the process.

She'd decided—for whatever reason so many years ago—that Gabriella wasn't a suitable partner for her son and she was going to do everything in her power to keep them apart. Apparently that included planting audio surveillance devices in Gabriella's home. When he confronted her, she neither denied nor apologized for her actions, insisting that she only wanted him to know what kind of vengeful, vindictive woman Gabriella really was.

Cameron had snapped the disk in half and told his mother to get out of his house. Then, when he'd verified that Gabriella and her mother and daughter were all out for the afternoon, he'd sent his own security team over to locate and remove the bugs. They'd found one in the kitchen, one in the living room, and one in Gabriella's bedroom.

On his way to Gabriella's house later that day, he tried to push all thoughts of Elena's lies and machinations from his mind. When Sierra opened the door and greeted him with a tentative smile, his heart actually felt as if it was expanding inside his chest.

And he finally realized that Gabriella was right—that the mistakes of the past didn't matter half as much as the gift of the present. Even though it was apparent that Sierra was ready to walk out the door as he was coming in, her smile confirmed that he was making progress with his daughter, and that was enough for now.

"Hi, Cameron. Bye, Cameron." She smiled again, then kissed her mother's cheek. "Bye, Mom."

But Gabriella held up a hand, halting her daughter's movement toward the door. "What's in the backpack?"

"My pajamas, toothbrush, a change of clothes."

"Because?"

"I'm staying at Jenna's tonight, remember?"

"I remember you asking if you could stay at Jenna's," Gabriella acknowledged. "And I remember telling you that I didn't think it was a good idea."

"Come on, Mom." Sierra cast a glance in Cameron's direction, as if to remind her mother that he was there, probably hoping she wouldn't want to argue in front of her guest.

But Gabriella shook her head. "Not tonight."

"Why not?"

"Because I wouldn't have any way of knowing what time you got back to Jenna's—or even if you did."

"I'll call you at midnight."

"No, you'll be back here by midnight," Gabriella insisted.

"You don't trust me," Sierra accused.

"If I didn't trust you, you wouldn't be going to the party at all," her mother told her.

"This is so unfair."

"Twelve o'clock," Gabriella said again.

"Do you realize that I'm the only one who has to be home by midnight?"

"Do you realize that I don't care what rules other parents set for their children? I only care about you."

"My life sucks," Sierra grumbled.

"I'm sure, from your perspective, it does," Gabriella agreed. "But for tonight, you have one of two choices. You can go to the party and be home by midnight, or you can not go to the party at all."

Sierra dumped her backpack on the ground. "Yeah, like that's really a choice."

"If you want to invite Paolo to come back here with you, I'm okay with that."

"Because Paolo's really going to want to leave the party at midnight."

"Obviously that's his choice."

"Yeah—*his* choice," Sierra repeated. "Because his parents don't treat him like a child."

"Maybe because he's eighteen years old and doesn't have temper tantrums like a child."

Sierra's eyes narrowed on her mother. She looked both angry enough and tempted to stamp her foot, but of course, that would only prove Gabriella right. Instead, the teenager turned on her heel and slammed the door as she went out.

Gabriella sighed, then turned to him with a rueful smile. "And that was the entertainment portion of the evening," she said lightly.

"Entertaining and enlightening," he said, matching her tone.

"Does it make you have second thoughts about wanting to take on the task of parenting a sixteen-year-old girl?"

"No," he said. "It only makes me admire you all the more."

"You're kidding."

He shook his head. "Every time I look at her, I'm absolutely awed and amazed to think that I had any part in her creation. But all I did was contribute to her DNA. And as stubborn and willful and downright scary as she can be at times, she's also a great kid, and that's entirely your doing."

Her smile wobbled, just a little. "Thanks. It's hard, some-times, trying to enforce boundaries for her own protection when she insists on pushing against them."

"Do you really think her request to spend the night at her friend's house was just a ruse?"

"I know it," she said. "Because I was a teenager once, too, and I came up with all kinds of excuses to stay out past my curfew or spend the night with a friend in order to be with you."

He frowned. "How old were you, exactly?"

"Seventeen."

He scrubbed his hands over his face. "You were barely older than that child who just walked out the door."

"I was old enough to know what I wanted," Gabriella assured him. "And you were everything to me. I would have done almost anything to be with you."

"I don't think I'd ever been as completely infatuated with anyone as I was with you," Cameron confided. "From the very first time my friends and I went into Marconi's and you walked out of the kitchen, weaving your way between the tightly packed tables with a pizza tray held over your head, I was smitten."

"You were obnoxious."

"Andre was obnoxious," he reminded her. "I was just desperate to get your attention."

She smiled at the memory. "You succeeded."

"I ate a lot of pizza over the next few weeks, just so that I'd have an excuse to see you and talk to you."

"I didn't mind—you never skipped out on your bill and always left a decent tip."

"And still, you kept refusing to go out with me."

"I didn't understand why you kept asking," she admitted. "It was so obvious to me that you were way out of my league."

"You were so beautiful." He stroked a hand over her hair, let his fingers sift through the silky ends. "You *are* so beautiful."

"And you're still way out of my league," she said, sounding regretful.

"Don't you remember how good we were together?"

"Good is a valuation," she hedged. "And I didn't have any experience to judge it against."

"Then you'll have to trust my judgment, and believe me when I say that we had fabulous chemistry."

"We're not kids anymore," she said. "And now we have a kid to think about, which makes this a lot more complicated now than it was all those years ago."

"So tell me to go." He dipped his head and brushed his lips against hers, softly, fleetingly. "Tell me to go, and mean it, and I'll turn around and walk right out that door."

The tip of her tongue touched her bottom lip. "I invited you to come for dinner," she reminded him. "It would be rude to tell you to go without even feeding you."

"I don't care about dinner."

"I was going to order Thai."

"Tell me to go," he said again. "Or ask me to stay. But be sure you know what you want."

He saw the indecision in her eyes. Desire warring with caution; hope battling with fear. He understood her hesitation. They were at a crossroads, and if they went forward from here, there would be no going back.

She lifted a hand, laid her palm over his chest where his heart was beating fast and hard against his ribs.

"You," she finally said. "I want you."

Then her hand slid up to cup the back of his head, drawing his mouth down to hers so that she could whisper against his lips, "Stay."

Chapter Fourteen

Cameron's heart pounded hard against his ribs. Once, twice, as his mind absorbed her response. "You're sure?"

He couldn't believe he was asking the question. But the first time, he hadn't given her a choice. He'd seduced her thoroughly and completely, so that she'd been incapable of refusing what he wanted, what he needed.

He needed her no less now, but he also needed to know that the choice was hers and one made freely and without hesitation.

"I'm sure," she promised, and held out her hand.

He linked his fingers with hers and let her lead him up the stairs to her bedroom. The door was open, as were the pair of windows that flanked the gaslight-style double bed, and light, gauzy curtains waved in the gentle breeze. On the opposite wall, there were two mismatched dressers, with photos of Sierra hanging above. He didn't take in any other details—he was focused only on Gabriella.

She'd paused in the center of the room, and was looking

at him uncertainly. He raised their still-joined hands to press his lips to her palm, and felt her tremble.

"I feel like I'm seventeen again," she said, her voice little more than a whisper. "The way my heart is pounding and my knees are shaking."

He pressed her palm to his chest again, so that she would know that his heart was pounding, too. "I feel as if I've been waiting for you forever."

His lips brushed over hers, softly, testing.

Her eyelids drifted down on a sigh.

He took his time. Even if this was what they both wanted, he didn't want to rush. Not this time. Instead, he lingered on her mouth, sampling, nibbling, savoring her uniquely exotic flavor. When he finally slid his tongue between her lips, a low hum of pleasure sounded in her throat, and he took the kiss deeper.

It was only when his hands moved to the top button of her blouse that she started to draw back.

"I should pull down the shades," she said.

"Why?"

"Because it feels strange to be taking my clothes off with the sun streaming in the window."

"You don't have any neighbors close enough to peek in," he said, brushing his lips against hers again. "And I want to see you. Every inch of you. Gloriously naked."

"Now I'm really nervous," she admitted.

"Only because you're thinking. So stop thinking," he instructed, and kissed her again.

It was a long, deep kiss that completely and effectively wiped all thought from her mind. She wasn't thinking anymore, she wasn't capable of thinking anymore, only feeling. She could feel her heart pounding, she could feel the heat that pulsed in her veins, and she could feel the desperate, aching need that spread through her body.

This time, when he started to unfasten her buttons, she didn't even think of stopping him. When he pushed the blouse off of her shoulders, the balmy air caressed her skin, raising goosebumps on her flesh. Then he wrapped his arms around her waist, pulling her tight against his body, and all she felt was heat.

He ran his hands over her shoulders, down her arms. She tugged his shirt out of his pants, anxious to touch him as he was touching her. Her hands fumbled, just a little, as she worked at his buttons. When she had most of them unfastened, he tugged it over his head and tossed it aside.

Her hands splayed over his chest, relishing the feel of solid, warm flesh beneath her palms, and the strong, steady beat of his heart. Her hands slid lower, tracing the hard ridges of his abdomen, then lower still.

Within minutes, they were both naked, but as eager as she was for the joining of their bodies, she didn't want to rush a single moment of their time together. Cameron must have felt the same way, because he didn't immediately move toward the bed but seemed content to keep kissing her, touching her, teasing her.

When he finally lowered her onto the bed, the old mattress protested with a creak and a groan that jolted Gabriella back to reality. What was she thinking—making love with him here? He was used to being with glamorous women in exclusive penthouse hotel rooms, making love on top of sheets that probably cost more than all of her bedroom furniture combined. He was a prince and she—

The thought drifted away as his hands stroked over her, shooting arrows of pleasure streaking across her skin. Yeah, he was a prince, but he was here with her now, and that was all that mattered.

He worked his way from the top of her head to the tips of her toes, exploring and arousing every single inch of her. He used his hands and his lips and his body until she was panting with want, aching with need, and willing to beg. He took her to the sharpest edge of pleasure and then, finally, over. Her body was still trembling with the aftershocks when he drove into her, sending a whole new wave of sensation crashing through her system. Her hands clutched at his shoulders, her legs anchored around his hips. She felt as if she could drown in the pleasure he was giving her, and she gloried in it.

She cried out, her nails digging into his flesh as her body tightened around him, dragging him into the storm of sensation along with her.

He held her in his arms. As the last of the sun's rays faded from the sky, plunging the room into darkness, he continued to hold her. Her head was nestled against his shoulder, her arm draped across his belly—until his stomach grumbled, loudly.

"We skipped dinner, didn't we?"

"I wasn't hungry before," he said, his hand stroking down her back. "Except for you."

She tilted her head back to look at him. "And now?"

"Now, I'm starving," he admitted.

So they ordered the Thai food she'd promised him earlier. Then, refueled and re-energized, they went back to her bedroom and made love again.

"I missed you," he said, somehow finding it easier to speak the truth in the darkness. "I don't think I realized how much until I saw you again."

"While I appreciate the sentiment—"

"You don't believe me," he guessed.

"Cameron, I went to see you less than a month after the weekend we spent together and you didn't even remember my name."

"That's not true," he told her. "I only pretended not to remember your name."

"Why would you do something like that?" He heard the skepticism in her tone and ached for the hurt he'd caused.

"Because I didn't want to admit—even to myself—how much you meant to me. In only a couple of months, you'd gotten under my skin, wholly and completely. When I got home after saying goodbye to you at the end of that weekend, all I could think about was seeing you again."

"And I'm supposed to believe that's why you never called?" she asked dubiously.

"I know it sounds crazy—"

She didn't deny it.

"—but you have to understand how unusual that was for me. I was a royal—and I'd become so accustomed to having women throw themselves at me, I felt as if that was a birthright as much as my title.

"You were different, right from the start. I'd never felt about anyone else the way I felt about you, and the depth of those feelings terrified me. I was sure that if I just took a step back, I'd realize you weren't any different from any other girl I'd been with."

"That's flattering," she said dryly.

"But I was wrong," he told her. "The longer I stayed away, the more I missed you. And the harder I tried to deny my own feelings. When you showed up at the college that day—I was so thrilled to see you, and equally determined to play it cool. And then, when you told me you thought you might be pregnant...well, that panic was very real."

"I was feeling a little panicked myself."

He stroked his hand over her hair. "I'm so sorry."

"I'm not," she said. "I was hurt and angry for a long time, but once I got past that—or mostly past it, anyway—I was more grateful than anything else. Because Sierra truly was a blessing. I was young and alone and terrified, but I knew I had to get it together for her. She gave my life a focus—everything I did, I did for her."

"You put your own life on hold to raise our daughter while I was raising hell around the globe," he realized.

"We each have our hobbies," she said lightly.

He brushed a strand of hair off of her cheek. "When is it going to be time for you?"

"Well, I kind of think *this* was for me," she teased, trailing a finger down his chest, then beneath the covers and lower still.

She closed her fingers around him, and his eyes nearly crossed. "Yeah, that's definitely for you," he told her.

"Show me," she whispered against his lips.

It was a request he couldn't—and didn't want to—refuse.

A sound from downstairs stirred Gabriella from the depths of slumber. Her eyes went automatically to the clock on the small table beside her bed, though she had to squint to focus on the glowing numbers. When the time finally registered, she jolted from half-asleep to wide-awake in two seconds, but it was two seconds too late.

"Mom?" Sierra's voice was followed immediately by her footsteps.

Gabriella swore and pushed back the covers. Her clothes were still scattered on the floor, so she grabbed her robe off the hook on the back of her door.

"I'll just be—"

She was going to say "a minute" but Sierra, accustomed to an open-door policy, didn't wait for the rest of her response but stepped into the room.

Gabriella had just finished fastening the belt on her robe, and her daughter automatically apologized. "I didn't think you'd be asleep already."

"I wasn't asleep. Not yet." She tried to move out of the room, to steer her daughter back into the hall before her eyes adjusted to the dark enough to realize that there was someone still in her mother's bed.

She didn't know if Cameron had awakened, but if he had, she trusted that he would quickly assess the situation and stay quiet until Sierra was out of the room. She didn't anticipate an untimely phone call.

"What was that?" Sierra asked, obviously not recognizing the ring-tone.

She blew out a breath. "Cameron's cell phone."

Sierra's jaw dropped open. "Cameron's here?"

Gabriella took her daughter firmly by the shoulders and steered her out into the hall.

"Oh. My. God." Sierra stared at her, obviously stunned and hurt and furious. "You are *such* a hypocrite."

"I'm an adult," Gabriella said sharply. "And I don't have to explain myself to you."

"So it's okay for you and Cameron to spend the night banging the headboard against the wall while I'm watching the clock at the party to ensure I'm home by my twelve-o'clock curfew because *you* don't trust *me* to stay out with my boyfriend any later than that?"

"That's enough, Sierra." It was Cameron who spoke this time, and there was steel beneath his quiet tone.

Sierra spun to face him. "This is between me and my mother. You have no right—"

"I have more rights than you know," he told her.

"Because you're a prince?" She practically sneered the question at him.

He met her gaze evenly. "Because I'm your father."

Sierra felt as if all the air had been sucked out of her lungs.

She stared at him, unable to think or breathe. She couldn't believe it—it couldn't be true. She looked to her mother, silently seeking confirmation—or maybe she was hoping that Gabriella would deny his outrageous statement.

"Is it—" She had to swallow. "Is it true?"

Gabriella glanced at Cameron. Sierra had been on the receiving end of that look often enough to know what it meant—it was a silent reprimand to him, and a wordless confirmation for her.

"Oh. My. God." She had to lean back against the wall because her knees were suddenly feeling too weak and trembly to support her.

"Why don't we go downstairs to talk about this?" Gabriella suggested.

Sierra didn't want to go downstairs. She didn't want to talk about it. She didn't want it to be true. And yet, while her brain scrambled desperately for any other explanation, the heart that had always ached for a father urged her to believe.

Gabriella put a hand on her daughter's shoulder. "Sierra?"

She pushed away from the wall and started down the stairs.

While Gabriella busied herself making tea, Sierra tried to wrap her head around the possibility that Prince Cameron Leandres might actually be her father. She shook her head. It was too outrageous to believe.

She waited until her mother had brought the pot and cups to the table, then she asked, "Are you sure?"

Gabriella's cheeks flooded with color. "Of course, I'm sure. I was never with anyone else."

She turned to Cameron. "So you seduced a virgin and then abandoned her when she got pregnant?"

"I wouldn't have described the situation exactly like that," he said, "but that's essentially the truth."

She was surprised that he didn't try to paint the facts to present his actions in a more favorable light. Surprised and wary. "So why are you here now? It's been sixteen years."

"Because I want a chance to get to know you, to be a father to you."

"And how is sleeping with my mother supposed to accomplish that?"

"Sierra." Her mother's tone was sharp, and the glance she sent in Cameron's direction this time was apologetic.

"Well, at least I know now why you were always so tight-lipped when I asked any questions about my father," Sierra said to her. "It would have been embarrassing for you if I'd gone to school in the second grade and told my friends that my father was a prince. I mean, who would have believed it?"

"I've always tried to be honest with you," Gabriella said.

"If you'd really wanted to be honest, you would have told me who my father was when I asked. Instead, I got a song and dance about how he was someone you'd known a long time ago, someone you really cared about but who wasn't ready to be a father."

"All of which was true," her mother insisted.

"And suddenly he's ready and I'm supposed to be the happy, dutiful daughter? Well, you can forget that," she said. "I don't want or need a father now."

"Whether you like it or not, I am your father," Cameron told her.

"I don't like it," she decided. "And the way I see it, you weren't really anything more than a sperm donor."

His eyes narrowed dangerously, and Sierra shifted in her seat, suddenly nervous that she might have pushed him too far.

That she might have pushed him away.

"I think it might be a good idea to continue this discussion another time," Gabriella interjected. "Maybe in a few days…"

"Maybe in a few years," Sierra muttered.

Gabriella sighed. "Why don't you go up to bed? We'll talk in the morning."

Sierra wasn't sure how she felt about being so obviously dismissed, but she was grateful for the opportunity to escape.

She needed time and space to get her head around everything. But as she moved into the hall, she heard Cameron say, "I'm leaving for Rome tomorrow."

"Rome?"

Sierra hesitated, because in her mother's single-word response, she heard both surprise and suspicion.

"That was my secretary on the phone earlier," he explained. "I had some meetings scheduled for the end of the month that needed to be brought forward to accommodate the prime minister's vacation."

"And he called you after midnight on a Saturday to apprise you of the details?" Gabriella asked skeptically.

Sierra was blatantly eavesdropping now, but she didn't care.

"I told him to let me know as soon as the plans had been finalized," Cameron explained.

"Well, then." Sierra heard the scrape of chair legs on the tile floor, could picture her mother pushing away from the table. "You should be getting home to pack."

"I'm sure my valet has taken care of that already."

"Of course," she acknowledged coolly. "I should have realized you'd have someone to take care of those kinds of details for you."

Cameron finally seemed to clue in that something was up. "Why are you mad at me?"

"I'm not mad at you," Gabriella said wearily. "I'm kicking myself for being an idiot. Again."

"You think I'm going to Italy because we slept together? I got what I wanted and now I'm leaving the country to get away from you?"

"It wouldn't be the first time."

"I thought we'd moved past this, Gabriella. Yes, I treated you badly. I was a selfish and self-centered twenty-year-old who didn't think about anyone else. As a result, I missed out on the first sixteen years of my daughter's life, and it's quite possible she will never forgive me for that. But right now, I'm trying to focus on the future rather than the past—a future that I want to spend with you."

Gabriella's only response was to ask, "How long will you be gone?"

He blew out a breath. "Three weeks. After Italy, I'm going to France then Germany and Switzerland."

Sierra took a step forward. She was still hidden in the shadows but could partly see into the room, and she saw Cameron take her mother's hands in his.

"Come with me," he said.

Gabriella blinked, clearly stunned by the invitation. "What?"

"Come with me," he said again. "We could ride in a Venetian gondola and climb to the top of the Eiffel tower, catch a performance at the Frankfurt Opera and visit the Palais des Nations in Geneva."

"I thought it was a business trip."

"If you came, it would be business and pleasure."

She shook her head. "I have responsibilities here, I can't just take off on a whim—"

"If you really wanted to, we could make it work," Cameron insisted.

She didn't respond.

He made his way to the door, paused with his hand on the knob. "Maybe I am the one who's leaving, but you're the one who's running this time."

Gabriella stared at the door for a long moment after he'd gone. When she finally turned away, Sierra fled, silently tiptoeing up the stairs, trying not to think about the tears she'd seen shimmering in her mother's eyes.

Elena had a copy of Cameron's itinerary on top of her desk, so she knew that he was already on his way to Rome. He had a welcome dinner with the prime minister later tonight and meetings scheduled for the next several days after that.

She had hoped that it wouldn't come to this, but her son had left her no choice. She picked up the phone and called Reynard.

"It's time to get this started."

Chapter Fifteen

Sierra hid out in her room most of Sunday. Katarina came home from her weekend with Dominic later that evening, and Gabriella stayed awake all night second-guessing her refusal to go to Italy with Cameron.

She'd never been to Italy. Actually, aside from one trip to New York City with Rafe, she'd never been outside of Tesoro del Mar. She frowned at the thought, surprised by the realization that it was the first time she'd thought of Rafe since she'd said goodbye to him more than three weeks earlier. She'd thought she was in love with him, she'd even considered marrying him, and less than a month later, she was twisted up in knots over some other guy.

Okay, so Cameron was more than that. He'd been her first lover, the first man she'd ever loved, maybe the *only* man she'd ever loved. And the man she *still* loved.

She dropped her head down on her desk, banged it against the wood, as if the action might knock some sense into her. How was that possible? How could she still love him? And how could she have only realized it now, after she'd sent him away?

If she'd had qualms about her decision on Sunday, it was nothing compared to the fears and uncertainties that began to nag at her when she saw the photo of Cameron and Bridget Dewitt in the paper on Tuesday.

She waited for him to call, but he didn't, and she wasn't sure what to make of his silence. He'd invited her along on his trip, she'd said no. Maybe he felt that they'd said everything there was to say. But dammit, they'd slept together the night before he'd left. He should have at least called to explain why he was cuddled up with some other woman less than forty-eight hours after he'd left her bed.

She knew that she was being irrational. If she really wanted to talk to him, to demand an explanation, she could call him. But of course she didn't.

She was relieved when he finally left Rome on Thursday. And then she saw the paper on Friday.

This time he'd been photographed at a cocktail reception for international delegates attending the trade summit in France. There were several recognizable faces in the picture—political leaders and international financiers—but her gaze was drawn immediately to Cameron and the statuesque blonde by his side.

If she didn't know better, she'd think he was courting the press, that he was angry with her for turning down his invitation and wanted her to know where he was and who he was with. Except that he didn't look like he was angry. He looked like he was immensely enjoying the company of the gorgeous woman by his side.

She tossed the paper aside and took her mug of coffee into her office.

She tried to put the photo out of her mind and concentrate on her column, but the words wouldn't come. Every response she tried to write sounded false, and she knew why. Because a woman who could screw up her own life so completely had no business trying to advise others about theirs.

The tap at the door was a welcome reprieve, and she smiled when Sierra poked her head into her office.

"Busy?"

Gabriella shook her head.

"Have you seen this?" Her daughter held up the morning newspaper as she stepped cautiously into her mother's office.

She nodded and lifted her mug to her lips, wincing as she sipped her now stone-cold coffee.

"Aren't you mad?"

"At whom?"

"Cameron," Sierra said, as if the answer should have been obvious.

Gabriella noted that her daughter had yet to refer to her father by anything other than his given name or his formal title. Obviously she was going to need some time to accept the familial relationship between them, and she silently cursed the inopportune timing of the prince's trip. Sierra was still reeling from the news that Cameron was her father, and Gabriella believed her daughter would have benefited from having him around to answer her questions, assuage her doubts.

"Honey, I know this is all new to you, but your—*Cameron*," she hastily amended, "has lived his entire life in the public eye. For a lot of women, being seen with a prince, having her name linked with his—however temporarily—is an enormous thrill."

"So it doesn't bother you that he was photographed with a redhead in Rome and a blonde in Bordeaux?"

Of course it bothered her. Enough that she'd taken the time to do some quick internet checking herself, which gave her the information to answer her daughter's question.

"He's on a business trip," she reminded Sierra. "The blonde happens to be an American ambassador also in France for meetings, and the redhead is an internationally-known model currently dating the youngest son of the Italian prime minister."

Sierra was silent, as if absorbing this information.

"You used to badger me with questions about your father," Gabriella reminded her. "If there's something you want to know now, just ask me."

"I guess I was just wondering…or maybe remembering. When I was little and asked you about my dad, you always told me that you'd loved him very much."

Gabriella nodded.

"Was it true?"

"Yes," she admitted. "I might not have given you a lot of information about your father, but what I did tell you was always the truth."

"Are you still in love with him?"

And because Gabriella didn't like to be dishonest with her daughter, even if she'd only recently acknowledged the truth to herself, she nodded again.

"So why didn't you go with him?"

She narrowed her gaze. "What makes you think he asked?"

"I heard him," she admitted. "When you told me to go to bed, I stayed in the hallway, listening to your conversation, and I heard him ask you."

There was no point in lecturing Sierra about eavesdropping on other people's conversations. What was done was done. So she only said, "Then you heard me tell him that I couldn't go because I have responsibilities here."

"That's a cop-out," Sierra said. "You know it and he knows it, too."

"I'm willing to answer any of your questions about Cameron but not about my personal relationship with him."

"Do you still have a personal relationship with him?" Sierra challenged.

Gabriella didn't have a ready response to that one.

* * *

Sierra hated keeping secrets from Jenna.

What was the point of having a BFF if she couldn't talk to her? But Gabriella had been adamant that she couldn't tell anyone about her father. Not even Jenna. Not yet.

But she had to talk to someone. And there was no one that she trusted more than Jenna. And she knew that she could trust her, because she'd told Jenna about the night she'd snuck out to meet Paolo, and Jenna hadn't whispered a word to anyone, not even Rachel or Beth.

So when she got home after her doctor's appointment Friday afternoon—without her cast finally—she picked up her phone and texted Jenna.

Can you get away? Need 2 talk 2 u.

And Jenna, because she was her BFF, texted back right away:

Where?

Half an hour later, they were sipping iced cappuccinos down at the waterfront.

It was only the beginning of the second week of a three-week trip, and Cameron already wanted to go home.

Usually he enjoyed the travel that was an essential aspect of his job, the opportunity to visit new places and meet new people. But in the short time that he'd been away, he'd realized that there wasn't anywhere in the world that he wanted to go unless it was with Gabriella and Sierra.

By the time he got to Germany, he was feeling edgy and impatient to be home. He thought about calling Gabriella. In fact, not a day had gone by since he'd left Tesoro del Mar that he hadn't picked up the phone at least half a dozen times to dial to her number. But each time, he'd set it down again. He wanted her there with him, but she'd refused. Of course, he'd been too stubborn and proud to beg, and now he was alone.

Well, not exactly alone. He was on his way to meet Dieter Meier for dinner. Dieter was the president of a major manufacturing firm in Nuremburg and an old friend from Cambridge, and Cameron was looking forward to catching up with him. But he promised himself that he would call Gabriella after his dinner with Dieter.

Except that when he got back to his hotel, there was a woman in his room. And not the woman he'd been missing.

"How did you get in here?" he demanded.

Chantal St. Laurent's glossy, painted lips curved. "I know the manager."

"Okay—what are you doing here?"

She rose to her feet, somehow balancing on four-inch ice-pick heels, and crossed the room to where he'd stopped, just inside the door. She'd poured herself into a short spandex dress that was the same color blue as her eyes. There were diamonds at her ears and her wrists, so that she glittered with every step and every turn. She looked good, spectacular even, but her presence stirred only basic male appreciation—and more than a little suspicion.

She ran a manicured nail down the front of his shirt, tracing the buttons. "Hoping to catch up with an old friend."

They used to run in the same circles, but he wouldn't have said they were friends. For a brief time they'd been lovers, but even then, they'd never been particularly friendly toward one another.

She slid her fingertip beneath the fabric, lightly scraped her nail against his bare skin. He grabbed her hand, pulled it away.

"I don't have time for your games, Chantal."

She pouted. "You just don't remember how much fun my games are."

"I do remember," he assured her. But mostly what he remembered was that she had a red-hot body and an ice-cold heart. "I specifically remember that you screwed me over more than you ever screwed me, and that wasn't a lot of fun."

"Let me make it up to you."

She tried to reach for him again, but he caught both her wrists and held her away.

"You can make it up to me by leaving this room. Now."

He dropped her wrists, but instead of going to the door, she moved toward the bar. She took her time selecting a glass, added a few cubes of ice from the silver bucket, then poured a generous splash of scotch over them.

She swirled the liquid around in the glass, then looked up at him with those big blue eyes that had brought legions of men to their knees. "Please don't send me away, Cameron. Not when I came all the way from St. Moritz to be with you."

He didn't ask what she'd been doing in St. Moritz. Truthfully, he didn't care. But he did wonder, "How did you even know I'd be here?"

"I've been following your career through the newspapers, hoping that our paths would cross again." She took a long sip of the scotch. "I've missed you, Cameron."

"Was I ever gullible enough to believe the lies that trip so easily off of your tongue?"

She set the glass down again with a snap. "You're not the man I remember."

"You have no idea how pleased I am to hear that," he told her.

"You'll regret turning me away," she promised him.

"I regret that you aren't already gone."

She picked up her glass again, tossed the last of her drink in his face.

He should have anticipated the attack. Unlike Allegra, Chantal had always been impulsive, her moods mercurial, and he'd baited her. Not because he wanted a reaction, but because he wanted her gone.

He was still blinking away the alcohol that stung his eyes when he heard the door slam. Well, he'd got what he wanted in that regard, anyway.

He flipped the security lock and went to the bathroom to shower off the remnants of expensive scotch and cheap memories.

Gabriella awakened to the sound of someone knocking on her door. No, it was more of a pounding, and the impatient, incessant hammering made her heart jolt painfully in her chest. It wasn't quite 4:00 a.m., and nothing good ever came from someone at the door at 4:00 a.m.

She pushed out of bed, yanking on her robe as she made her way down the stairs. She grabbed the phone from the charger on the way to the door, in case she needed to call 9-1-1. A flick of the switch had light flooding the front porch and revealing the identity of the late-night visitor.

She flipped the lock and yanked open the door.

"Alli? What on earth are you doing here?"

"I came to save you from the media hounds that will be on your doorstep before sunrise."

"What are you talking about?"

"The news just came across the wire," her editor warned her. "Alex saw it and immediately called me at home."

Her heart jolted again. "What news?"

"About Sierra."

"What about Sierra?" Katarina demanded.

Gabriella and Alli both turned to find Katarina on the stairs, Sierra behind her.

Alli glanced past Gabriella. "That she's Prince Cameron's daughter."

Gabriella didn't waste her breath swearing. She'd known the

truth would come out eventually and while she wasn't happy about the timing, she didn't think it was cause to panic— although apparently her editor did.

"The presses are running overtime," Alli told her. "But the print media's only part of it. The story's already all over the internet. There are photo montages on YouTube and blog posts about your affair."

Okay, so she hadn't expected the truth to come out quite like this. She swallowed, hard, as her stomach muscles cramped into painful knots.

"What can I do?" she asked.

"Go pack a suitcase," Alli advised, her gaze shifting to encompass both Katarina and Sierra in her instruction.

"I'm not letting the paparazzi chase me from my home," Gabriella's mother said.

"Hopefully it will only be for a few days," Alli soothed.

"And where are we supposed to go?" Sierra demanded.

"There's nowhere we can go that the reporters and photographers won't find us if they're determined to do so," Gabriella acknowledged dully.

"Actually, there is one place," Alli said.

"Where?"

"The royal palace."

Gabriella stared at her, certain her friend had lost her mind. "Okay," she said, playing along. "Let me just call the prince regent to see if there are any vacancies in the castle."

"No need," Alli told her. "I already did."

"You can't be serious."

"Prince Rowan and I go way back...to the beginning of June when you wrote that story about his cousin and the daughter of the King of Ardena, anyway."

"You really called him?"

"He's sending a car and bodyguards to make sure you get from here to there without incident."

"Well, then, we should get dressed," Katarina suggested, finally starting back up the stairs. "We can't go to meet royalty in our pajamas."

It was impossible not to be impressed by the royal palace. But as her daughter goggled over the marble floors and crystal chandeliers and her mother inspected the heirloom vases overflowing with fresh flowers and family portraits in ornate frames on the walls, Gabriella found herself even more impressed by the graciousness of Rowan Santiago, the prince regent, and Princess Lara, his wife, who both came to the foyer to greet them when they arrived.

Gabriella automatically dipped into a curtsy, and her mother and daughter followed suit.

"Please," Lara said, taking her hand. "It's an ungodly hour to worry about such formalities."

"It's an ungodly hour to be anywhere other than bed," Rowan added, "and your rooms are ready for you."

"Thank you, Your Highness," Katarina said gratefully.

"Hannah—" he gestured to the woman who hovered in the background "—will show you the way."

Sierra stifled a yawn as she fell into step beside her grandmother. Gabriella stayed back.

"I don't imagine sleep will come easily with everything that's on your mind," Lara said gently to her. "But you should try to get some rest."

"I will," she agreed. "I just wanted to thank you. I know those words are grossly inadequate, and I'm sorry that we showed up at your door under such circumstances, and so very grateful that you've opened your home to us."

Rowan put an arm across his wife's shoulders, a casual gesture of comfort and affection. "She's going to change her mind in a few hours."

The knots of anxiety that had begun to loosen when the driver pulled through the palace gates tightened in Gabriella's stomach again, but she forced herself to ask, "What's going to happen in a few hours?"

Lara smiled. "The kids will be awake."

The sun was high in the sky and the vultures were circling when Cameron's plane landed at the Port Augustine airport.

He was surrounded by bodyguards as he made his way from the plane to the car, but still he felt the press of the paparazzi pushing in on him. He ignored the shouted questions, the deliberately provocative comments and the blinding flash of cameras. He had only one focus: getting to Gabriella and Sierra.

He knew they were at the royal palace, and that they were safe there. But he didn't know if they had seen *El Informador*.

His secretary had handed him a copy of the paper as he'd stepped onto the plane, and after he'd read and reread the outrageous article, he'd spent the remainder of the almost three-hour flight thinking about how badly he'd screwed everything up.

As he ducked into the back of the black Mercedes SUV and the vehicle slowly began pulling away from the media mob, he accepted that Gabriella would have seen the article. It was inevitable, really. What worried him was that she might believe it.

Rowan and Lara's two sons were very spirited and utterly adorable. Matthew was six-and-a-half, William was almost four, and when the three generations of Vasquez women met them at breakfast the next morning—along with seventeen-year-old Princess Alexandria and thirteen-year-old Prince Damon—they were all immediately charmed. Prince Christian had eaten with Rowan much earlier, Lara informed her guests, so that they could indulge in a morning ride before the demands of the day caught up with them.

The boys chatted up a storm while Gabriella nibbled on a piece of toast and sipped her coffee, and for a few blissful minutes she let herself forget why she was hiding out at the palace and simply enjoyed being there.

When Lara slipped away to take a phone call, Katarina excused herself to head out to the gardens and Lexi invited Sierra to join her for a swim, leaving Gabriella with three very handsome—and very young—members of the royal family. By the time Lara returned, the boys had finished their breakfasts and gone down to the stables and Gabriella was indulging in a second cup of coffee.

"Should I apologize for everyone abandoning you or are you savoring a few quiet minutes?" the princess asked.

"I'm savoring," Gabriella admitted. "Probably because I know it's the calm before the storm."

"Did you manage to get any sleep last night?" Lara asked gently.

"Some," she said. "Enough that I'm thinking a little more clearly this morning and wondering if it wouldn't just be better to face the press and get it over with so that they move on to something else? And I think, if I was the only one who would face the backlash, I would do it."

"You're worried about your daughter," Lara guessed.

She nodded.

"I hope she doesn't mind staying here for a few days. I know kids—teenagers in particular—can be particular about their own space."

"Mind?" Gabriella smiled. "She said she feels like a princess."

"She is a princess," Lara reminded her.

"I know," she admitted. "But I'm not sure Sierra has let herself acknowledge that fact."

"Because it would mean accepting that Cameron is her father," the princess guessed.

Gabriella nodded. "It hasn't been an easy time for Sierra.

She hasn't known about Cameron very long—I thought I was doing her a favor, by keeping the identity of her father a secret. Because I knew that if anyone found out she was his daughter, her life would change." Her smile was wry. "Obviously I screwed up there."

"No one can blame you for wanting to protect your child," the princess said. "Although I don't know if it's fair—or even possible—to protect her from her birthright."

Gabriella sighed. "I know."

"But speaking of Cameron—he should be arriving here shortly."

"He's back from Germany?"

"His plane landed about twenty minutes ago."

Gabriella winced. "I can't imagine he's pleased to have his trip interrupted to deal with this media frenzy."

"I wouldn't worry," Lara said. "I'm sure Cameron is more accustomed to seeing his name in the headlines than most people."

"Does that mean... Is it in the headlines today?"

The princess nodded and passed her a copy of *El Informador*.

"*La Noticia* covered the basic story, too," Lara told her. "They couldn't very well be the only newspaper in Europe that ignored it, but they reported only the facts that had been independently confirmed."

Gabriella didn't reply, her attention already snagged by the harsh words spread across the top of the front page.

Chapter Sixteen

Prince Cameron's Mistress Exposes Truth About His Secret
Love Child With Another Woman

Former international supermodel Chantal St. Laurent, recently spotted snuggling with the Tesorian prince in Germany, stormed out of his hotel room in Munich early this morning after learning that her lover is the father of an illegitimate teenage daughter with newspaper columnist Gabriella Vasquez.

"I was shocked when he told me," she later confided to a friend.

Independent investigation has confirmed that Gabriella Vasquez is the mother of a sixteen-year-old daughter named Sierra, but the prince is not named as the father on the child's certificate of birth. In fact, the official document lists the father as "unknown." Sources close to

Ms. Vasquez at the time of her child's birth agreed that she was uncertain about who had fathered her child.

Gabriella pushed the paper aside, unable to read any further. And the thought of Sierra being exposed to such ugly lies and rumors—she felt sick just thinking about it.

"It's a gossip rag," Lara said gently. "And Chantal St. Laurent will say or do anything to see her name in print. I don't know how she happened to be in Germany at the same time as Cameron, but I promise you it wasn't a coincidence."

"You think she set him up?" she asked hopefully.

"I think she's spewing venom and lies," Lara said. "I can't imagine what she thinks she'll gain from any of this, but I don't doubt for a minute that she made up the whole thing."

"Even the part about being in his hotel room?" she asked hopefully.

"No, she was there."

Cameron acknowledged the fact wearily as he stepped into the room.

He looked exhausted, as if he'd been up all night. Exhausted but still so handsome, and Gabriella wanted to rush into his arms. She wanted him to hold her and reassure her that everything was going to be okay. But she knew that he couldn't make that kind of promise and it was foolish and naive to wish that he could—especially when he'd just admitted that the woman who'd sold out Sierra to the media had been in his hotel room. With him.

"I was out for dinner with a friend," he explained, "and when I got back to my hotel room, Chantal was there."

"*In* your room?"

He nodded. "She wasn't there very long—probably not more than ten minutes. Just long enough to ensure that the photographer was in place to snap the photo of her leaving again."

"And long enough for you to tell her about Sierra,"

Gabriella said, though she was still trying to fathom why he would do so.

"I didn't say a word to Chantal about Sierra," he said.

"Then how—" Gabriella faltered, as the pieces finally clicked into place in her mind.

Cameron nodded. "I knew you'd figure it out."

Lara picked up her coffee cup. "Is anyone going to fill me in?"

But Gabriella shook her head, wanting to deny it. "I know she hates me, but this—the lies and innuendos—they're going to hurt you and—" she blinked back the tears, because she knew that if she let even a single one fall, she wouldn't be able to stop the flood "—Sierra as much as they hurt me."

"Collateral damage," he said easily. "The princess royal wouldn't concern herself with that so long as she got what she wanted."

Lara stared at Cameron. "You think *your mother* set this whole thing in motion?"

"She didn't want Cameron to ever know about Sierra," Gabriella told her.

"And since you failed to keep that information from me, she used it to hurt you."

"Wait a minute—" the princess turned to Gabriella "—are you saying that Elena knew about Cameron's child and didn't tell him?"

"Yes, she knew," Cameron admitted.

Lara shook her head and pushed away from the table. "Apparently you two have bigger issues than the paparazzi to work through, so I'll leave you to it."

Cameron sat down at the table across from Gabriella.

"Are we going to be able to work through them?" he asked softly.

She wanted to say "yes." She wanted to believe it was true. But she wasn't as naive or idealistic as she used to be and she knew that the odds were stacked against them. It wasn't just that he was a royal and she was a commoner; it wasn't even that their fledgling relationship was suddenly under very public scrutiny. It was so many different things, but mostly it was the acceptance that no matter how much she loved him, love wasn't always enough.

And so, when she finally responded to his question, it was to say, "I honestly don't know."

It wasn't the answer he wanted, but Cameron couldn't blame Gabriella for being cautious.

One step forward, two steps back, he thought wearily. Their relationship had finally been moving in the right direction, until he'd left the country with a lot of questions and uncertainties still between them.

"Are you…" she hesitated, almost as if she was afraid of the answer he would give to her question. "Is it true—" she started again "—about you and Chantal being lovers?"

"No," he said. "*Dios,* no." And it was the truth, but not the whole truth, and he knew that he couldn't hold anything back from Gabriella now. If they were going to move forward, they couldn't do so with any more secrets between them. "Not anymore."

"So you were," she murmured.

"A long time ago."

She nodded.

She didn't look surprised or even disappointed. Obviously his confirmation was no more than she'd expected, and why wouldn't it be? For a lot of years, he'd been known as the partying prince—a favorite of the paparazzi because he was always out on the town, always with a different woman, always having fun. He'd grown weary of the scene long before he'd managed to extricate himself from it, and though he'd done so more than half a dozen years earlier, the reputation continued to haunt him.

"If it was over a long time ago, why would she do this?" Gabriella gestured to the paper.

He had several theories about the unlikely partnership between his mother and his former lover. It was possible that Elena had bribed or blackmailed Chantal to ensure her complicity. It was just as likely that Chantal had jumped at the opportunity to be involved—just for fun. "Because Chantal's never as happy as when she's in the middle of a scandal."

Gabriella shook her head. He knew she didn't understand people like Elena and Chantal, people who could find pleasure in using their power to hurt others. Her basic honesty and goodness had appealed to him from the start. And even when he'd been furious with her for keeping his daughter a secret, he'd known that it hadn't been easy for her.

Elena, on the other hand, wouldn't have lost a wink of sleep over the role she'd played in the deception. More likely, she'd have taken pride in the display of her power. It was what she did—manipulating others so that she could feel important. He'd long since figured out that her behavior was rooted in her own childhood, in the feeling that she was insignificant and powerless because she was a female child born to a ruler who already had a male heir. But the fact that he'd come to understand the reasoning behind her behavior didn't mean it sickened him any less.

Gabriella turned the paper over, so that she didn't have to see the headline staring at her. "Sierra's going to be devastated when she sees this."

Cameron wasn't so sure. Oh, he knew that Sierra would be hurt, that she'd wonder if there was any truth in the midst of all of the lies. But the fallout for her would be minimal. Regardless of what anyone believed about her father or her mother or the circumstances of her conception, she was the innocent in all of this. Right now he was more concerned about Gabriella.

"Rowan suggested a press conference, and I agree that it's probably the best way to handle this," he told her.

"Why don't I just walk outside the palace gates with a target on my chest instead?"

He reached across the table to touch her hand. He half-expected her to pull away, and when she didn't—when she actually turned her hand to link their fingers together—the relief he felt was almost overwhelming.

"We're going to present a united front," he promised her. "Me and you and our daughter. We'll read a prepared statement and formally introduce Princess Sierra and we won't answer any questions."

"That won't stop them from asking."

He nodded, acknowledging the fact.

"Okay." She drew in a deep breath. "When are we going to do this?"

They decided that the press conference would be held at Waterfront Park at nine o'clock the next morning. The exact location wasn't too far from where Cameron had initially confronted Gabriella about Sierra's paternity, although that was by coincidence rather than design. Rowan's advisors had suggested the outdoor stage where summer concerts often took place as a suitable venue to ensure access to all the media who chose to attend. Cameron had some concerns about providing security for Gabriella and Sierra in such an open space, but the prince regent promised that the royal security detail would be there to look out for them.

Gabriella had hoped that the paparazzi would back off when the date and time of the conference were announced. As grateful as she was to Rowan and Lara for allowing them to stay at the palace, she wanted to be back in her own home, she wanted to pretend that things were normal. But the media vans remained just outside the palace gates, trapping her inside.

When she'd ducked out of her house under cover of darkness

so many hours earlier, she hadn't thought about what she was throwing into the bag she brought with her. She certainly hadn't packed anything that would be appropriate to wear to a press conference. She had no sooner expressed this concern to Lara than the princess asked if she wanted to make a list of items for someone to pick up from the house or do some online shopping. Though she was tempted by the shopping, she opted to make a list. She already owed the princess far more than she could ever repay.

An hour later, she was sorting through the suits and blouses she'd selected. She managed to narrow it down, but continued to waver between the taupe and the red.

"Definitely the red," Lara said, when she'd finally got up the nerve to ask the princess for her opinion. "Even if you wear the taupe, you won't be able to escape the spotlight but it'll look like you tried. Also, Sierra's wearing red. Red and white, actually, but you'll coordinate nicely. And red is definitely your color."

So the next morning, Gabriella got dressed in the red, then she went to see what her daughter was wearing.

She halted in the doorway of Sierra's room and absorbed the twinge of regret that stabbed at her heart when she couldn't see any sign of her little girl anywhere. Instead, there was a poised and beautiful young woman in front of her, dressed in a simple but elegant white sundress with red poppies dancing along the hemline, red peep-toe pumps on her feet and a wide-brimmed red hat on her head.

"It was Lexi's idea," she said. "The hat. She said it would make me look more mysterious."

"I almost didn't even recognize you," Gabriella said with a smile.

She was pleased that Alexandria and Sierra had hit it off so quickly. Lexi had been raised as a princess from birth, so she knew everything there was to know about the duties and responsibilities of a royal and had already proven herself an invaluable support to Sierra.

"You look fabulous."

She smiled shyly. "I feel strange. I mean, I like the outfit, it's just so different from my usual style. But Lexi said it set the right tone between formal and casual."

"It's perfect," Gabriella assured her.

Sierra nodded. Then she took a deep breath and blurted out. "I told Jenna. About Cameron being my father."

And Gabriella suddenly realized why her daughter had been so uncharacteristically quiet and withdrawn over the past two days—not just because she was feeling overwhelmed by everything that was happening, but because she was feeling guilty.

"She's my best friend," Sierra continued. "And I didn't think she'd tell anyone—"

"She didn't," Gabriella interrupted. She took her daughter's hands, squeezed gently. "The leak didn't come from Jenna."

"You're sure?"

She nodded. "There were…details given to the media that Jenna couldn't have known, that you didn't know."

Sierra exhaled a heartfelt sigh of relief. "I thought this was all my fault."

"Oh, Sierra." She hugged her daughter tight. "None of this is your fault, honey. If anyone's to blame, it's me. If I'd told you the truth—if I'd told Cameron the truth—a long time ago, we might have avoided this now. Or at least been more prepared for it."

"Well, I'm as prepared as I'm going to be," Sierra told her. "So let's get it over with."

The park was packed. Somehow word had got out that Prince Cameron's daughter was going to be in attendance and the citizens of Tesoro del Mar flocked to the park, anxious to finally set eyes on Princess Sierra. A lot of Sierra's friends were there, too. Aside from Jenna, no one had known that her father was a prince until they'd read it in the papers or seen it on television, and they were all curious to know if the prince's daughter really was the same Sierra Vasquez that they knew.

Gabriella wasn't surprised by the turnout. She'd known there would be more curiosity-seekers than media personnel, but she'd still tried to discourage her mother from attending, worried that Katarina would be an easy target for the paparazzi. But Katarina had insisted on being there to support her daughter and granddaughter, and Gabriella saw that she wasn't alone. In fact, she was flanked on all sides by members of Cameron's family. Rowan and Lara and Matthew and William; Christian and Lexi and Damon; Eric and Molly and Maggie and Joshua. Even Cameron's sister, Marissa, was there, with her other brother's daughter.

Only the princess royal was absent—apparently having left the country on short notice to visit an ailing friend in Corsica. Gabriella knew that explanation was nothing more than an excuse, but she was nevertheless as grateful for Cameron's mother's absence as she was everyone else's support.

As a child, Sierra had relentlessly hounded Gabriella for a sister or a brother, and Gabriella's heart had ached that she couldn't give her little girl what she wanted. What Gabriella, too, had always wanted. Because from the time she'd been a child, she'd dreamed of someday having a big family—including at least half a dozen kids running around the yard.

Of course, in that scenario she'd also imagined that she would have a husband—someone who went out to work at a respectable but normal nine-to-five job every day and came home to his wife and family every night. Falling in love with a prince had totally screwed up all of her plans, and while she could maybe forgive herself for the youthful fantasies that had allowed it to happen when she was seventeen, she should have known better this time around.

...the mind does not and cannot control the heart.

She no longer doubted the truth of her mother's words, but as she looked out at the familiar faces in the front row, she could at least be happy that she'd finally given her daughter the family that she always wanted.

Rowan's secretary stepped up to the microphone first, drawing her attention back to the purpose of the assembly. He introduced himself to the crowd, thanked everyone for coming, and announced that Prince Cameron had a statement to make.

Though neither Gabriella nor Sierra was expected to say anything, it was agreed that they would stand with Cameron, demonstrating their support of him and agreement with the official statement he would deliver.

"Over the past couple of days, the media has been inundated with rumors regarding my history with Gabriella Vasquez and the paternity of Gabriella's daughter, Sierra. I'm here today to separate the fact from fiction..."

Gabriella didn't listen to any more of his speech. They'd gone over it together the previous afternoon, so she knew exactly what he intended to say. Instead, she focused on the sound of his voice, allowing her frayed nerves to be soothed by the smooth cadence.

As he spoke, she held Sierra's hand in her own. Her daughter's icy fingers were the only outward indication of her trepidation. She had to know that everyone was staring at her, but she stood tall with her head held high, looking every inch the princess, and Gabriella had never been more proud.

There was a brief silence after Cameron finished speaking—probably not more than a few seconds—and then the real uproar began. There were so many questions that it was almost impossible to decipher any individual words, until someone shouted: "Prince Cameron, are you going to marry Gabriella?"

And Gabriella's heart actually stopped for the space of several beats.

She and Cameron had talked about this scenario and they'd agreed that they wouldn't respond to any questions or statements from the crowd. But this one seemed to linger in the air for a moment, as if everyone was waiting for an answer. As Gabriella held her breath, waiting for the same thing.

Cameron had heard the question. She had no doubt about that. And he even paused, as if considering his response. But in the end, he only said, "Thank you all for your time."

And then he turned away from the microphone.

Sierra immediately fell into step behind him, obviously eager to get off the stage and away from the endless flash of bulbs, and Gabriella followed her. There were still questions being shouted, but Gabriella was only aware of the one that had gone unanswered.

What did you think—that he'd want to put a ring on your finger? Wake up, Gabriella. You're a nobody from nowhere and he'll never marry you.

The words that echoed in her mind now weren't those of her mother but his, and the scornful tone with which they'd been delivered had cut her to the quick. Because she'd believed him when he'd told her he loved her, and she'd been foolish enough to think that a man who loved her would want to marry her.

She wasn't seventeen anymore, and yet, she'd let herself get caught up in the fairytale all over again. She'd fallen in love with Cameron and she'd trusted him when he'd told her that he wanted a future for them together. She'd believed that he was committed to her and their relationship, but his silence on the subject of marriage spoke volumes.

Behind the scenes, the security force was filling vehicles for the return trip to the palace. Sierra rode with Lexi and her brothers, and Katrina had climbed into a vehicle with the prince regent and his family, leaving Gabriella to ride with Cameron.

She settled back against the plush leather seat with dark-tinted windows and finally let herself breathe. No one could see her in here. No one could know that her heart was breaking. No one except Cameron—but he'd seen it all before.

She didn't realize the tears had spilled over until she felt the brush of Cameron's knuckle on her cheek, wiping them away. His touch was gentle but she felt as if a fist was squeezing around her heart, and the ache was both painful and real.

"Are you okay?" he asked.

She nodded. "I'm just relieved it's finally over so I can go home." Back to her own house, her own life. Reality.

"It wouldn't hurt to stay at the palace a few more days," Cameron said. "You heard the questions the reporters were shouting—they don't have all the answers they want yet."

"Yes, I heard the questions," she agreed.

"We knew it was going to be like that," he reminded her. "No matter how much information we gave them, it wouldn't be enough."

She nodded. "I know. It wasn't the questions that bothered me—not really."

"Then what was it?"

He sounded as if he really didn't know, and she had no intention of enlightening him. "I understand that the media attention is a fact of life for you, and I know it will be for Sierra, too, but I can't live like that."

"What, exactly, are you saying?"

She drew in a deep breath. "That I don't want a life in the spotlight so we should stop pretending that a relationship between us could ever work."

His gaze narrowed on her. "At seventeen, you were pregnant and washing dishes in a restaurant kitchen so that you could afford to buy a crib for your baby. After you had the baby, you took night courses and you worked your way up from the circulation desk to columnist at *La Noticia*. I think you've already proven that you can do just about anything you want to, so if you think you can't handle a few skirmishes with the media, maybe the truth is that you don't want to," he accused.

"Maybe I don't," she agreed. "Or maybe I just don't want to handle it all by myself."

He scowled. "What are you talking about? You weren't by yourself. I was right there—"

"Standing on the opposite side of Sierra." She felt tears stinging her eyes again. "As if she was the only connection we had."

"What was I supposed to do—announce to the crowd that we're lovers?"

The words were a knife straight through her heart, the final, fatal strike to her illusions. She'd thought they were so much more than lovers. She'd thought they were in love, planning a future together, building a family.

"No," she finally said. "You weren't supposed to do anything."

Cameron followed her out of the SUV and up to her room, where she immediately began tossing her things into a suitcase. "If you're going to be mad, you could at least tell me why."

"I'm not mad."

It was obviously a lie, but he knew better than to call her on it. "Okay, then tell me how to fix whatever it is that I screwed up."

"There's nothing to fix," she said. "I've just decided that I won't be your dirty little secret anymore."

"What the hell are you talking about?"

"That's how Chantal referred to Sierra, but the truth is, our daughter was simply the result of your youthful indiscretion. You have absolutely nothing to be ashamed of there.

"But it's not quite so easy to explain me, is it? And that's why you haven't even tried. That's why you're so careful not to be seen in public with me, and why, even today, you kept six feet of space between us."

"How can you blame me for trying to shelter you from the media when you said you didn't want your name linked with mine in the tabloids?"

"That was before we were sleeping together."

"Well, obviously I didn't get the memo about the rule change."

"You had a chance to stand with me today," she told him. "To show the world that you wanted to be with me, to tell them 'yes—I do plan to marry her.'"

He couldn't help it. Afterward, he would agree that was no excuse for his action, but it was purely reflexive, completely instinctive—he stepped back.

She turned away to zip up her suitcase.

"Come on, Gabriella," he said reasonably. "We've only been together for a few weeks."

She looked right at him, baring her true feelings. "I know. But I've loved you for seventeen years."

I've loved you... If you loved me... The words spun in circles in his mind, making him dizzy.

He didn't want to believe that she was trying to manipulate him. He knew that she wasn't like that. And yet, he'd listened to those words too many times, and hearing them fall from her lips now, he froze.

"Are you giving me an ultimatum?" he asked coolly, waiting for her to spell out her terms. Waiting for her to look at him, her eyes filled with pleading/fury/tears, and finally tell him what she wanted. What he needed to do to prove that he loved her.

But she didn't look at him at all. She only picked up her suitcase and said, "No, I'm leaving."

Chapter Seventeen

It was rare for Cameron to have visitors at his office. And his days were usually so tightly scheduled that he wouldn't have time to spend with anyone who just happened to drop by, anyway. But since he wasn't yet supposed to be back from his trip, he had large blocks of unscheduled time—most of which he spent thinking about Gabriella and how thoroughly he'd ruined everything.

So when his secretary buzzed through on Tuesday afternoon to tell him that someone was there to see him, Cameron was grateful for the reprieve. Even more so when he realized that his visitor was Sierra. He hadn't seen her since the day of the press conference—the day that Gabriella had walked out on him.

He hadn't seen Gabriella, either, but only because he had yet to figure out the best way to grovel for her forgiveness.

"Lexi told me that it would be okay if I stopped by," Sierra said. "She didn't tell me I'd have to present three pieces of ID and be subjected to a body scan in order to get past the front door."

"I'll make sure you get security clearance so you can come here any time you want without going through all of that again," Cameron told her.

"That might be a good idea," she agreed. "Since I've decided that I should probably get to know you a little better—because of the family connection thing."

"I'd like that," he said.

"But it would be a lot more convenient for me if you came around to the house again," she told him.

"I could talk to your mother about the possibility," he said cautiously.

"Or you could just show up," she suggested. "I know she'd be happy to see you."

"Well, I'm not so sure about that."

She huffed out a breath. "Are all guys so dense?"

"I'll assume that's a rhetorical question," he said dryly.

"Okay, answer this one—are you in love with my mother?"

"Yes."

She blinked. "Wow. Not even a moment's hesitation."

"I would have told her the same thing, if she'd given me a chance." At least, he wanted to believe he would have told her, but she'd started talking about commitment and he'd started feeling backed into a corner.

He'd lived his whole life with his mother pulling his strings until he'd finally severed them. And then he'd been both relieved and determined that no one else would ever have that power over him again.

Unfortunately, it wasn't until Gabriella had gone and he'd listened to himself pouring his heart out to Lara that he realized Gabriella had never tried to bend him to her will. She wasn't looking for a commitment at any cost. She only wanted him if he wanted her, too.

And he did want her—more than anything else in the world.

"That's good, but the words aren't going to be enough," Sierra warned him. "She needs to know that you're going to stick."

"What do you mean?"

"You've got a history, right? She fell in love with you when you were younger, you said you loved her, too, and then you were gone. Fast-forward sixteen years and some months, and you're back again, saying you love her, blah-blah-blah."

"Blah-blah-blah?"

"I'm trying not to think too much about the details," she told him. "It's kind of weird, you know, with her being my mom and you being my dad."

She said it casually, as if it was no big deal, but to Cameron, it was a very big deal. It was the first time she'd explicitly acknowledged their father-daughter relationship, and while he was tempted to haul her in his arms and hug her so tight she could barely breathe, he managed to restrain himself.

"Your point?" he prompted instead.

"It's easy to say you love her, but she needs you to prove that you mean it."

"And how, exactly, am I supposed to do that?"

Sierra smiled. "Why are you asking me for advice when you could go straight to the relationship expert?"

Dear Gabby,
I'm writing to you in the desperate hope that you can help me convince the woman I love of my feelings for her.
    I'm a thirty-six-year-old man who has fallen in love only twice—both times with the same woman. The first time, I was barely twenty years old, too young to understand the depth of my feelings and too immature to appreciate how truly rare and special our love was.

The second time was much more recent. After more than sixteen years apart, our paths happened to cross again and I realized that the feelings I had for her so long ago had never gone away.

I've tried to show her how I feel, but I think she's afraid to believe it, afraid that I'll hurt her again.

I'm more than willing to put my heart on the line. I'd happily hire skywriters or put a message on the big screen at a baseball game—whatever it takes to let her know that I'm going to stick around this time... forever.

Should I set my plans in motion—or do you think a man who royally screwed up once doesn't deserve a second chance?
Signed,
Lost in Love

Gabriella reread the letter twice. At first, she hadn't let herself believe Cameron had written it, but there were too many specific details to be able to disregard. And while hope flared in her heart, she forced herself to tamp it down. Because despite what he said in the letter, nothing had changed.

Or maybe everything had changed. The princess royal had told her that Cameron would never marry her, but this letter suggested not only that he would but that he wanted to, that he really wanted to be with her forever.

With that cautious hope in her heart, she settled her hands on the keyboard and began to type.

Dear Lost,
While I believe that everyone makes mistakes and everyone deserves second chances, I'd hold off on hiring the skywriters. Your willingness to put your heart on the line in a very public way is admirable, but not every woman wants or needs such a big statement. In fact,

some women might worry that a man who goes to such extremes might be more flash than substance.

Instead of shouting your feelings from the rooftops, take the time to show her what's in your heart. As cliché as it sounds, it's often the little things that mean the most. Pick her a bouquet of flowers. Hold hands. Walk with her in the rain. Cook her favorite meal. Call her at bedtime, just to say good-night.

Give her some time to see and believe that you intend to stick around forever. It's not easy to let go of past heartaches, so be patient, be understanding, and be there for her.

Good luck,

Gabby

It happened to be raining the day that his letter and her response appeared in the newspaper, so Cameron snuck out of the office during his lunch and dropped by Gabriella's house. His wipers were on full-speed to clear the water from his windshield, giving him a moment's doubt about his plan, but he didn't change his course.

Gabriella was obviously surprised to see him, and more than a little wary when he suggested that she should put her coat and shoes on. But when she finally did, he took her by the hand and walked with her in the rain. They didn't go far but they still ended up soaked through to the skin.

He called her later that night, to see if she'd managed to dry out yet and to say good-night.

The next night, he called her again. And then again the night after that. He never kept her on the phone for more than a few minutes—just long enough for him to let her know that he was thinking about her and, he hoped, to make sure that she was thinking about him.

On the fourth night, he invited her to dinner. And after only a moment's hesitation, she accepted.

* * *

Gabriella was a nervous wreck as she got ready for her date with Cameron. Of course, it didn't help that both her mother and her daughter were hanging out in her room, critiquing every outfit that she tried on. Too sexy. Too frumpy. Too young. Too old. Finally Katarina left to go to her hot yoga class, and when Jenna called to see if Sierra wanted to go out for an iced capp, Gabriella was relieved to shove her daughter out the door, too.

Cameron showed up a short while later, with an enormous bunch of flowers in his hand. There were tall spikes of lavender, cheery pink anemones, fat white lilies and bobbing Spanish bluebells. But what she noticed, after the gorgeous array of colors, was that the stems of the flowers were uneven and broken…almost as if he'd picked them.

"They're beautiful," she said, filling a vase with water. "But I'm not sure why you're doing this."

"Doing what?"

"Bringing me flowers. Taking me to dinner."

"Because I don't cook, either," he told her. "I wanted to make your favorite meal, but I only know how to make reservations."

She smiled at that. "It wasn't intended to be a checklist, you know, just a few suggestions."

"But those suggestions made me realize that we'd missed a lot of those basic getting-to-know-you rituals and I thought it was time we started following some more traditional conventions."

"Such as?"

"Well, dating usually precedes courtship which precedes marriage."

The vase slipped out of her hands and clattered into the sink, splashing water all over the counter and Gabriella.

He handed her a towel. "And marriage, of course, precedes children. Obviously, we've done some things backwards."

She dabbed at the wet splotches on the front of her dress. "Backwards implies a reverse order, but we actually skipped a couple of those steps."

"We'll get to them," he promised.

"Is that was this is about? Are you…courting me?"

"And apparently not doing a good job of it, if you have to ask."

She looked at the flowers again. She could only imagine where he'd picked them—probably from a stranger's garden—and her heart completely melted. "Actually, I think you're doing a wonderful job."

"Really?" he asked hopefully.

"Really." She set the vase on the counter, then turned to touch her lips to his cheek. "Thank you for the flowers."

"You're welcome," he said, and kissed her again.

It was a kiss filled with hunger and frustration and longing, and Gabriella responded with her whole heart.

After what seemed like an eternity and yet not nearly long enough, he eased away. He brushed his thumb over her bottom lip, a slow sensual stroke that made her tremble. His eyes darkened and, for just a moment, she thought he was going to kiss her again.

Instead, he took a step back. "We should get going. We have a reservation at Tradewinds."

She drew in a long, slow breath and nodded. "Right. We wouldn't want to miss our reservation."

But neither of them moved.

"Although we've never worried much about conventions," she reminded him.

"No," he agreed.

"So maybe, instead of sitting through dinner wondering if the evening will end with sex, why don't we start with sex and wonder if we'll make it to dinner?"

He drew her back into his arms, which was exactly where she wanted to be. "I really like the way you think."

* * *

It was a long time later that he looked at the clock beside her bed and said, "We missed our dinner reservation."

She sighed contentedly. "We could order pizza."

"Okay." He kissed her. "One question first."

"Pepperoni," she told him, belting her robe.

He rummaged around on the floor, looking for his pants. "That wasn't the question."

"Okay, what's the question?"

He found his pants and put them on. Apparently whatever the question was, he didn't want to ask while he was naked. Then he shoved his hand into the pocket and pulled out a small, square box. Her heart began to pound furiously inside her chest.

"Compared to the sixteen years that we were apart, we've only been together for a short while," he said. "But the past two weeks without you have been the longest weeks of my life and I don't want to live another day without you by my side."

She blew out an unsteady breath. "You sure moved through that courtship stage fast."

"Because I finally realized what I want. And that's to marry you, build a life and share a family with you, Gabriella."

She desperately wanted to throw her arms around him and tell him that she wanted that, too. But while her heart was already committed, a tiny part of her brain continued to urge caution.

"Your mother hates me," she reminded him. "And to be honest, I'm not too fond of her either."

"I've gone through this scenario a few times in my mind," he admitted. "And never once did I imagine you wanting to talk about my mother."

She managed a smile, though everything inside of her was a quivering mass of nerves and uncertainties. "She's not my favorite topic of conversation, but she's your mother—your family—and you have to know that she won't be happy about this."

"She'll adjust," Cameron insisted. "Because she knows that I won't tolerate her interference in my life ever again. She'll even come to the wedding and smile, because she's a princess and she understands the importance of duty."

The steel in his voice was reassuring, but she still felt compelled to ask, "Is that why you're doing this? Because you think that marrying the mother of your child is your duty?"

"I'm asking you to marry me because I love you," he said. "Because I've always loved you, even when I was too much of an idiot to realize it. And because I want you to be my family—you and Sierra…and maybe another baby."

Her heart stuttered. "A baby?"

"If that's what you want," he hastily amended. "If you don't want to do it again, that's okay. But—"

"I'd love to have another baby," she told him.

"Really?"

"Maybe it's crazy, considering that I'm now twice the age that I was when I had Sierra, but yes, really."

"Does that mean you'll marry me?"

"I haven't actually heard a proposal," she said.

So he went down on one knee beside the bed and flipped open the box. "Will you marry me, Gabriella?"

She didn't even look at the ring—she didn't need to. The love that she saw shining in his eyes was all that she needed to see. "Yes, Cameron, I will absolutely marry you."

He slipped the ring on her finger. "You realize that after we exchange vows you'll become a 'princess' and living outside of the spotlight will no longer be an option?"

"I can handle it." She wrapped her arms around his neck. "I can handle anything as long as you're by my side."

"Then that's where I'll be," he promised her. "Forever."

Epilogue

PRINCE CAMERON TO WED THE MOTHER OF HIS CHILD?
by Alex Girard

That's what everyone has been asking since the prince publicly confirmed he was the father of Gabriella Vasquez's sixteen-year-old daughter, Sierra, earlier this month. The question was finally answered on Saturday night in a beautiful candlelight ceremony at the royal palace.

The bride wore a simple but elegant Nicole Miller floor-length gown of ivory silk and carried a hand-tied bouquet of white gerbera daisies. The groom was outfitted by Savile Row in traditional black tie with royal decorations. The couple exchanged vows before an intimate gathering of family and close friends in the rose garden.

At the conclusion of the ceremony, the prince and his bride joined their hands together to cut into the gorgeous three-tier wedding cake created by the mother-of-the-bride (and having indulged in a taste of that exquisite cake, I now understand why Dominic Donatella wants to get his hands on her recipe!).

As the guests ate cake and drank champagne, Princess Sierra offered a first toast to the newlyweds, wishing them a long, happy life together—and wanting to know if they were *ever* going to give her a brother or a sister.

While the blissful couple left that question unanswered, at least for the moment, there is no doubt that their daughter's other wishes for them will come true.

* * * * *

*Look for Prince Michael's story,
the next book in Brenda Harlen's
REIGNING MEN miniseries.
Coming soon to Silhouette Special Edition!*

COMING NEXT MONTH

Available February 22, 2011

#2101 MARRIAGE, BRAVO STYLE!
Christine Rimmer
Bravo Family Ties

#2102 MENDOZA'S RETURN
Susan Crosby
The Fortunes of Texas: Lost...and Found

#2103 TAMING THE TEXAS PLAYBOY
Crystal Green
Billionaire Cowboys, Inc.

#2104 HIS TEXAS WILDFLOWER
Stella Bagwell
Men of the West

#2105 SOMETHING UNEXPECTED
Wendy Warren
Home Sweet Honeyford

#2106 THE MILLIONAIRE'S WISH
Abigail Strom

REQUEST YOUR FREE BOOKS!
2 FREE NOVELS PLUS 2 FREE GIFTS!

SPECIAL EDITION
Life, Love and Family!

YES! Please send me 2 FREE Silhouette Special Edition® novels and my 2 FREE gifts (gifts are worth about $10). After receiving them, if I don't wish to receive any more books, I can return the shipping statement marked "cancel." If I don't cancel, I will receive 6 brand-new novels every month and be billed just $4.24 per book in the U.S. or $4.99 per book in Canada. That's a saving of at least 15% off the cover price! It's quite a bargain! Shipping and handling is just 50¢ per book in the U.S. and 75¢ per book in Canada.* I understand that accepting the 2 free books and gifts places me under no obligation to buy anything. I can always return a shipment and cancel at any time. Even if I never buy another book, the two free books and gifts are mine to keep forever.

235/335 SDN FC7H

Name _____ (PLEASE PRINT)

Address _____ Apt. #

City _____ State/Prov. _____ Zip/Postal Code

Signature (if under 18, a parent or guardian must sign)

Mail to the Reader Service:
IN U.S.A.: P.O. Box 1867, Buffalo, NY 14240-1867
IN CANADA: P.O. Box 609, Fort Erie, Ontario L2A 5X3

Not valid for current subscribers to Silhouette Special Edition books.

Want to try two free books from another line?
Call 1-800-873-8635 or visit www.ReaderService.com.

* Terms and prices subject to change without notice. Prices do not include applicable taxes. Sales tax applicable in N.Y. Canadian residents will be charged applicable taxes. Offer not valid in Quebec. This offer is limited to one order per household. All orders subject to credit approval. Credit or debit balances in a customer's account(s) may be offset by any other outstanding balance owed by or to the customer. Please allow 4 to 6 weeks for delivery. Offer available while quantities last.

Your Privacy—The Reader Service is committed to protecting your privacy. Our Privacy Policy is available online at www.ReaderService.com or upon request from the Reader Service.

We make a portion of our mailing list available to reputable third parties that offer products we believe may interest you. If you prefer that we not exchange your name with third parties, or if you wish to clarify or modify your communication preferences, please visit us at www.ReaderService.com/consumerschoice or write to us at Reader Service Preference Service, P.O. Box 9062, Buffalo, NY 14269. Include your complete name and address.

USA TODAY *bestselling author Lynne Graham*
is back with a thrilling new trilogy
SECRETLY PREGNANT, CONVENIENTLY WED

Three heroines must marry alpha males to keep
their dreams...but Alejandro, Angelo and Cesario
are not about to be tamed!

Book 1—JEMIMA'S SECRET
Available March 2011 from Harlequin Presents®.

JEMIMA yanked open a drawer in the sideboard to find
Alfie's birth certificate. Her son was her husband's child.
It was a question of telling the truth whether she liked it or
not. She extended the certificate to Alejandro.

"This has to be nonsense," Alejandro asserted.

"Well, if you can find some other way of explaining how
I managed to give birth by that date and Alfie not be yours,
I'd like to hear it," Jemima challenged.

Alejandro glanced up, golden eyes bright as blades and
as dangerous. "All this proves is that you must still have
been pregnant when you walked out on our marriage. It
does not automatically follow that the child is mine."

"'I know it doesn't suit you to hear this news now and I
really didn't want to tell you. But I can't lie to you about it.
Someday Alfie may want to look you up and get acquainted."

"If what you have just told me is the truth, if that little
boy does prove to be mine, it was vindictive and extremely
selfish of you to leave me in ignorance!"

Jemima paled. "When I left you, I had no idea that I was
still pregnant."

"Two years is a long period of time, yet you made no
attempt to inform me that I might be a father. I will want
DNA tests to confirm your claim before I make any deci-

sion about what I want to do."

"Do as you like," she told him curtly. "*I* know who Alfie's father is and there has never been any doubt of his identity."

"I will make arrangements for the tests to be carried out and I will see you again when the result is available," Alejandro drawled with lashings of dark Spanish masculine reserve.

"I'll contact a solicitor and start the divorce," Jemima proffered in turn.

Alejandro's eyes narrowed in a piercing scrutiny that made her uncomfortable. "It would be foolish to do anything before we have that DNA result."

"I disagree," Jemima flashed back. "I should have applied for a divorce the minute I left you!"

Alejandro quirked an ebony brow. "And why didn't you?"

Jemima dealt him a fulminating glance but said nothing, merely moving past him to open her front door in a blunt invitation for him to leave.

"I'll be in touch," he delivered on the doorstep.

What is Alejandro's next move? Perhaps rekindling their marriage is the only solution! But will Jemima agree?

*Find out in Lynne Graham's
exciting new romance
JEMIMA'S SECRET*

*Available March 2011
from Harlequin Presents®.*

Start your Best Body today with these top 3 nutrition tips!

1. **SHOP THE PERIMETER OF THE GROCERY STORE:** The good stuff—fruits, veggies, lean proteins and dairy—always line the outer edges of the store. When you veer into the center aisles, you enter the temptation zone, where the unhealthy foods live.

2. **WATCH PORTION SIZES:** Most portion sizes in restaurants are nearly twice the size of a true serving and at home, it's easy to "clean your plate." Use these easy serving guidelines:
   - Protein: the palm of your hand
   - Grains or Fruit: a cup of your hand
   - Veggies: the palm of two open hands

3. **USE THE RAINBOW RULE FOR PRODUCE:** Your produce drawers should be filled with every color of fruits and vegetables. The greater the variety, the more vitamins and other nutrients you add to your diet.

Find these and many more helpful tips in

YOUR BEST BODY NOW

by

TOSCA RENO

WITH STACY BAKER

Bestselling Author of
THE EAT-CLEAN DIET

Available wherever books are sold!

NTRSERIESFEB

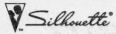

ROMANTIC

SUSPENSE

Sparked by Danger, Fueled by Passion.

CARLA CASSIDY

Special Agent's Surrender

There's a killer on the loose in Black Rock,
and former FBI agent Jacob Grayson isn't about
to let Layla West become the next victim.

While she's hiding at the family ranch under Jacob's
protection, the desire between them burns hot.
But when the investigation turns personal,
their love and Layla's life are put on the line,
and the stakes have never been higher.

A brand-new tale of the

Available in March wherever books are sold!

Visit Silhouette Books at www.eHarlequin.com

SRS27718